SHATTERED SINNER

BRENTSON UNIVERSITY SERIES
BOOK 5

BRI BLACKWOOD

BRETAGEY PRESS

NOTE FROM THE AUTHOR

Hello!

Thank you for taking the time to read this book. Shattered Saint is a dark college billionaire brother's best friend enemies-to-lovers romance. It is not recommended for minors and contains situations that are dubious and could be triggering. The book also includes underage drinking, binge drinking, stalking, and graphic violence. It isn't a standalone and the book ends in a cliffhanger. The next book in the series is Shattered Reign.

BLURB

This was never a part of the plan....

My life was in shambles.

My parents tried to seal my future to a man I didn't know.

But he could never have my heart.

It belonged to the one man who was forbidden to me, my brother's best friend.

Too bad he had no issue shattering it into a million pieces.

When I thought things couldn't get worse, my best friend was missing, leaving behind a void filled with dark questions and secrets.

The only thing I could do is fight for my survival.

I refused to be a pawn in this twisted game.

Welcome to my descent where I have no problem bringing everyone down with me.

PLAYLIST

Castle (The Huntsman: Winter's War Version) — Halsey
Radioactive — Imagine Dragons
Helium — Sia
Take Me to Church — Hozier
Heathens — Twenty One Pilots
human — Christina Perri
Heart By Heart — Demi Lovato
Look What You Made Me Do — Taylor Swift
Runnin' — Adam Lambert
Skyfall — Adele

The playlist can be found on Spotify.

1

BIANCA

Fear and dread flooded my veins as I sat in front of my father's desk. I was as still as a statue other than the slow blinking of my eyes. I was reeling from his announcement as I tried to justify how those pictures fit the bullshit crime he was saying I committed. My eyes were the only thing that moved as they analyzed the mysterious pictures spread across his desk. I wanted to glance at the rest of them, but I was afraid of drawing more attention to the problem at hand. Instead, my thoughts whirled around as I tried to think of how I could get out of this mess, and all the while, my eyes were drawn to the dark clouds that had formed in the sky.

"How could you do this?" I asked as my voice trembled. Every word tasted bitter, and I felt nothing but betrayal.

"How could I do this? This is all because of you!" my father exclaimed. The glare in his eyes did nothing but piss me off further. "This is what we need to do to protect our family's reputation and to smooth over this dent in my political career. You should be thanking me for cleaning this up."

"Thanking you? For trying to force me to marry Tristan Whitmore?" I scoffed as anger boiled beneath the surface. "I won't marry someone that you choose just because you want to save your career. Even though that's all you fucking care about."

"Watch your mouth," my father snapped back. "You've gotten us into this situation, and you will get us out. You *will* marry Tristan, and that's final."

Tears stung my eyes at the finality of his words. His voice was cold and matter of fact, feeling like a slap in the face to me. I struggled to keep myself from crying in front of him. He didn't deserve to see me cry or to be in the same room as me, frankly. This was too much to handle. For some reason, I couldn't believe that my own father would betray me like this. Then again, why should I be surprised that he was forcing me into a loveless marriage for the sake of his political career? I'd grown to expect that my father was an asshole, but this was beyond my wildest dreams.

Or should I say nightmare?

It was clear that nothing mattered as long as he got his way.

I couldn't give in to this. This was a battle of wills that shouldn't even exist. Surrendering wasn't an option for me.

Suddenly my fury couldn't be contained. It was as if my body thawed at once. There was nothing but fire in my heart, and the urge to fight him every step of the way. I jumped out of my chair, and I saw red. "I don't consent to any of this, so the only way I'm marrying that fucker is if I'm dead."

"What did I say about watching your language? And that's pretty rich when I'm the one that sustains your lifestyle, Bianca. So, once again, you're going to marry him, and that will be the end of this. Now if you'll excuse me, I have some guests I need to entertain."

He walked out of the room without another glance in my direction and almost slammed his office door behind him. I was sure once he stepped outside, he put on his picture-perfect smile and started shaking hands as if nothing was wrong.

Yet I was still in here, feeling as if my world had completely fallen apart.

My gaze landed on the window as a drop of rain hit the glass. I had to admit it was comforting to see that the weather outside mirrored how I felt on the inside. I took a deep breath to try to calm myself because I knew I needed to focus on thinking clearly. A plan was necessary in order to get through this.

But when my stare landed back on his desk, I couldn't take my eyes off the photos staring up at me. My nails dug into my palms after I clenched my fists, serving as a reminder of the reality that I was in.

The only explanation for this leak was Easton. These were the exact same photos he'd shown me on his phone, and now, because I ended whatever the hell we had going on, he decided to enact his revenge.

A wave of hurt crashed over me as I battled through the treacherous sea of my emotions. I tried to take small breaths to stop myself from sobbing, but I wasn't sure if I was success-ful. Whatever connection Easton and I had was now a twisted, convoluted mess, and I hated him more than I had over the last two years.

I rubbed both of my hands down my face before I glanced down at my father's desk and found a photo that hadn't been the focus of my deepest nightmares. Staring back at me was a photo of my parents, Nash, and me, which must have been taken on the same day the one that I had of us was. Our poses and expressions were slightly different—our smiles weren't quite as wide—but still, the happiness that we used to share shined through.

Too bad that was no longer the case.

Without another thought, I walked to the door. There was no doubt in my mind that I needed to get out of this room and fast. The walls in here were closing in on me, and the air was slowly starting to suffocate me, which told me that a panic attack could be incoming.

I needed to get out of here, right now.

I yanked open my father's office door, the squeaking of the door on its slightly rusted hinges did nothing but annoy me as I left the room. I ignored everyone around me as my feet propelled me toward the front door. Any sense of decorum had flown out the window, and I wouldn't be liable for how I might react if someone tried to stop me. It wasn't until I walked outside that I realized what I needed: fresh air.

The heaviness of my rage slowly left my body in the evening air. Should I have grabbed a coat before I left the house? Given that on any normal day during this time I would have been shivering, but today, my body felt as if it was burning from the inside out. I didn't make an attempt to cover myself because it was no use. At least the coolness from the raindrops helped soothe my soul. The rain had picked up slightly, but hadn't turned into a full-blown storm. Not that any of that mattered because even if Mother Nature decided that today would be the apocalypse, I was getting out of this house.

No one stopped me as I walked down the stairs and out to my car. No one bothered to call as I drove away from my parents' home and headed back to my place. The ride back was a complete blur. However, it wasn't until I stumbled into my apartment that I truly felt as if I could take a deep breath without feeling as if I was struggling under the weight of everything. The lingering scent of the vanilla candle that I lit while I was getting ready to head to my parents' home normally would have made me feel warm and fuzzy, but I felt anything but.

I threw myself onto the couch and closed my eyes, shoving everything I could out of my mind. The photos, Easton, my father's proposal, and Tristan. It took everything within me to push past the last couple of days, but I somehow managed. Nothing else mattered but me.

That lasted all of five seconds.

I lifted my body from the couch, and it took more effort than it should have. I strolled into my bedroom, much slower than I would have normally. I wasted no time in taking my clothes off my body. I was this close to ripping the offending garments from my body because, in the moment, it would have made me feel better even if it wasn't wise. I tossed on some sweats and walked back into my living area, where my eyes immediately landed on the half-empty bottle of wine on the counter.

That could take the pain away.

I walked over and grabbed the bottle before I took a long swig of the liquid. There was nothing quite like it, but I couldn't help but be annoyed that I wasn't drinking anything stronger. This wasn't the first time I'd used alcohol to place a warm blanket over my feelings, but not even it could calm the whirlwind of thoughts that were colliding in my brain.

What the hell was I going to do?

I walked back to my coffee table and set the bottle down in its new resting place before I sat down on my couch.

My pro-con list would be an excellent addition to this conversation, but I couldn't get myself to think of any reason for or against each side. Instead, I took another gulp of my wine before I sat back on the couch.

If I were to go through with this marriage, what would it be like? One thing I knew for sure was that I wasn't ready to be a wife, especially not to someone I barely knew. But... ending up on someone else's arm would make Easton see red.

It was a foolish thing to think about.

There was nothing I could do right now except to take another long drink of wine. And that I did.

2

BIANCA

I counted to ten before I walked into my psychology class. I tried everything I could to calm the nerves that were on the fritz. This had been the moment I'd been dreading since the last time I saw Easton, and now there was an even bigger issue I needed to deal with that he was also to blame for.

I made my way toward my usual seat, but there was something more unsettling about this moment. I could feel Easton's eyes on me, watching my every move. I chose to ignore him, instead focusing on one of my classmates, who'd given me a smile. I was hoping he'd take the hint and leave me alone. That was a silly thought because, of course, he had no intention of doing so. He leaned in, and I instinctively moved my body away from his.

"Hey. We need to talk."

I didn't bother to look at him because what was the point? The only thing that looking at him would do was bring on more pain. "No, we don't."

"We will talk after class," he said.

I balked at his demand. "No, we won't."

I could hear the wheels in his head turning as he tried to find a better way to approach this situation. "Bianca, it wouldn't take much for you to—"

"Easton," I interrupted sharply as I turned to face him. He wasn't going to manipulate this situation and force me to do anything. "There's nothing left to say, so fuck off."

He looked confused for a moment, but I turned away before my brain focused on dissecting it further. The last thing I wanted to do was focus on how he might be feeling because that meant reliving everything that happened. Hell, I still hadn't processed what I was feeling. I also had more important things to worry about, like, I don't know, finding out where my best friend was and getting married to basically stranger.

I watched as Dr. Chen walked into the room, a welcome reprieve from Easton's questioning or desire to talk to me. When she started speaking, I tried to focus on the words coming out of her mouth, but my mind kept wandering. Not to mention the heavy pull I felt toward Easton which served as a reminder of everything that was left unresolved between us.

"Miss Henson?"

I jumped as Dr. Chen's voice brought me back to the present. I turned to see her standing behind me. After realizing that I'd been daydreaming, a warm flush began to cover my cheeks because now I was embarrassed.

"Is everything okay?" she asked, a confused expression covering her face.

I forced a smile and said, "Everything's fine." I felt slightly guilty about lying. Everything felt wrong, but there was no way that I was going to answer any questions pertaining to what happened, especially in public.

"You look as if you're in pain," she said as I could hear the genuine concern in her tone.

I didn't know whether I should be offended that she said those words or not. I wanted to crawl under this desk and hide. Not only did I have her eyes trained on me, but I had to deal with Easton, and I wasn't sure if he'd stopped staring at me since I walked into the room.

When my throat felt as if it was being constricted, I knew there was no way I was going to be able to keep pretenses up. The lump in my throat grew larger as tears welled up in my eyes. It had been a long time since anyone had asked how I was doing.

"It's... personal," I said. My voice was barely above a whisper, and I wondered for a second if she'd heard me. The fact that I was able to say something at all was a miracle.

"Would you like to be excused from class?" she asked.

It took a moment for me to see the light, but when I recognized the opportunity, I snatched it. "Thank you, Dr. Chen. I appreciate it. I'm going to go talk to one of the therapists here at Brentson."

"I think that's the right solution," she said as she placed a hand on my shoulder. "If you need something else, let me know."

"Thanks," I said as I watched her walk away.

I could feel Easton's eyes on me as I threw my things into my bag and stood up. I didn't want to give him an opportunity to try to stop me. I could feel all eyes on me as I walked out of the classroom with my head held high. That lasted only for a moment because of the grasp on my arm.

I gasped as I turned around to see who grabbed me. My heart pounded in my chest as my gaze landed on the person standing behind me. I yanked my arm away and glared at the man looking back at me.

"Go back to class, Easton!" My words came out as a scream, surprising even myself. I reminded myself that I needed to keep my voice down because I was going to draw attention to us.

Easton didn't move a muscle, as his gaze didn't move from me. It felt as if he was daring me to do something. I tried to calm down so that he wouldn't realize how angry he was making me. I could see the amusement in his eyes, and I hated it.

"If this is the only way I'm going to get a chance to talk to you, then I'm willing to take it."

"I asked you to leave me alone and I mean it. Leave me the fuck alone, Easton." If my actual words didn't make it obvious, the irritation in my voice should have.

I looked around for a split second to make sure that no one was in the hallway. Most people who might have been wandering around this academic building were in class or so far away from us that they weren't paying attention to the confrontation we were having.

"You're only bringing attention to yourself, and Dr. Chen is probably wondering what the hell is going on with you now."

"I don't give a damn."

"Maybe you should because I do. I also have more important shit to do than to talk with you. Take a hint and leave me alone. If you make a move to touch me again, I'm going to scream, and we wouldn't want that now, would we?"

Before he could respond, I turned on my heel and walked away. A sliver of confidence appeared as I pushed my shoulders back and left Easton standing there.

"This isn't over, Bianca. You can bet on that."

His words sent a shiver through my entire body, and I hated it. I knew that his words were a promise he intended to keep. I let them wash over me as I walked out of the building. I stepped into the cool autumn air that was quickly turning into winter. The deep breath that I was able to take without Easton being near, allowed me to release some of the tension causing havoc in my body. This felt like freedom, even if it was only temporary.

I unlocked my car door and slid into the driver's seat with a needy sigh. I turned on some emo music because that was what I was feeling in the moment, and I drove back to my place. There was some guilt in my mind about lying to Dr. Chen about seeing a therapist. Deep down, I knew that I should go talk to someone about... well everything, but I wasn't ready. Whether I ever would be was another question entirely, and I honestly didn't know.

As soon as I was in my apartment, I slammed the door closed behind me and dropped my book bag on the floor near my counter. I didn't bother with pretenses and immediately went to pour myself some vodka into a glass. I was doing it to partially numb the pain I was feeling, but to also give myself something to do.

To make myself feel slightly better, I threw a couple of ice cubes into the glass, to dilute the liquor a bit as I was drinking it. But this time, the alcohol did little to mask my pain, yet I couldn't bring myself to stop.

By my second drink, I was shaking my head at myself. "I need to get my life together," I mumbled.

Yet I didn't take the words to heart. I spent the rest of the day drinking, unable to escape the burden I'd been forced to carry. There had to be something I could do, but my thoughts didn't make any sense. What I did know was I needed to find a way out of all of this, even if I had no idea how right now.

I turned on the television and curled up into a ball on my couch after I grabbed a blanket to lay over my body. Darkness started to take over my vision and my thoughts became convoluted. Leaving all of this behind circled my brain quicker than the alcohol flowing through my system.

As I started to feel sleepy, I whispered, "Tomorrow. Tomorrow is when all of this will make sense."

But my gut told me that was a lie. None of this was that simple and questions about whether I would be able to face any of this rose to the surface.

I was truly and utterly fucked.

THE NEXT DAY, I woke up to a throbbing headache and a queasy stomach. It wasn't shocking to me given the nature of what I'd been doing the previous day, but that didn't make how I was feeling any better. The room spun around me, making me dizzy. I was foolish to try and sit up, but when I did, the sudden movement made me want to vomit, so I laid back down on the couch.

"Ugh," I groaned, as I tried to keep my eyes open. I quickly accepted defeat and closed my eyes due to the light from the sun shining in and my hangover. "Why did I do this to myself?"

The real question was why I continued to do this to myself, but we would address that problem another day.

I glanced at my end table and saw that drunk me was apparently very smart and left a bottle of water and aspirin on the table. I swallowed two pills with help from the water. Either way, there wasn't much I could do other than rest and hydrate myself as I hoped the medication would kick in quickly.

I slowly made my way to my bathroom and sighed when my eyes narrowed due to the bright light and landed on my reflection in the mirror. I closed them again, trying to give myself the time to adjust to the brightness that surrounded me.

My eyes were bloodshot, the bags underneath them seemed to be growing darker purple and heavier by the second. My hair was a hot, tangled mess, sticking out of the messy bun I'd placed it in the night before. I was embarrassed by the complete and utter wreck in front of me.

"I look like I went a couple of rounds with a garbage truck and lost," I mumbled as I splashed cold water on my face. That didn't do much to stop the nausea or the pounding in my head.

The next stop was the shower. I turned on the showerhead, and after waiting for the water to heat up, I hopped in. I wasn't sure if it was the aspirin kicking in, the shower, or a combo of the two, but the pain in my head lessened a bit and I was grateful. I felt more human, but I still wasn't a hundred percent.

Once I was dressed, I grabbed a cup of coffee and found

some leftovers from the food I'd apparently drunk ordered yesterday. I pulled out my phone to call Iris. I'd grown to expect the outcome because it was the same one I got every time I called Iris.

The phone didn't even ring before it went to voicemail.

"Great," I sighed as I hung up. "Just fucking great." I stared at my phone, wondering what the hell I was going to do next. I missed my best friend, and this wasn't normal for her. For something like this, I would usually go to my brother and ask for his advice, but I was still pissed at him for the deal with Easton. My dad was an asshole, and while my mother hadn't been in the room when my father told me about my new "fiancé," I knew she more than likely agreed with him.

I needed to face this alone.

I did a double take as an idea appeared in my mind.

I was going to find Iris myself if it was the last thing I did.

3

BIANCA

I shivered as I set my sights on my destination. I got the creeps every time I thought about Westwick University, let alone stepped foot on campus, but I would do anything for Iris.

Even I had to admit that my half-baked attempt at trying to find Iris was foolish, but that wasn't going to stop me from doing it. Luckily for me, the drive to Westwick University was short, not giving me enough time to talk myself out of it. After I parked my car at Payne Hall, the first problem I needed to solve was how the hell I was going to get into the building.

Since I didn't attend Westwick, I didn't have an ID for the college that would potentially give me access to the building. Based on what I'd heard Iris say, not many people chose to stay at Payne Hall, and based on what I could see from the outside, I didn't blame them one bit.

The black iron gate standing near the entrance of the building had some rust on it and green moss covered parts of the building's gray brick walls. This dormitory gave off haunted vibes. No, the whole campus did.

I still didn't understand why Iris willingly chose to live here or go to Westwick when she could have easily applied somewhere else, including Brentson.

It seemed as if today might be my lucky day, because as I was walking up to the front door of the dorm, it opened, and someone held the door for me as I walked inside. Getting in had been easier than I planned, and maybe I would be able to call this whole search off pretty quickly.

I quickly found the stairs that would lead me to Iris's floor. I took them two at a time and soon found myself standing in front of her door. Without another thought, I turned the doorknob.

"Locked," I sighed, leaning my forehead against the cool wood of the door. "Of course it is."

I knocked hard on the door, and my anxiety grew as I waited for a moment to see if anyone would respond, or if I heard any noise coming from the room. When neither option panned out the way I hoped, I knocked again, louder this time, and received the same result. Nothing.

My heart began to pound in my chest, and it wasn't from the million stairs I had to climb to get to her room. The panic that I'd done my best to tame this morning began to surge. Where was Iris?

Desperately, I pulled out my phone to call Iris's number once again. "Come on, pick up," I said, wishing that was the password that would give way to me hearing Iris's voice.

"Are you looking for Iris?"

The voice came from behind me, making me spin around quickly because I hadn't been expecting it. The person asking was around my age, with deep brown eyes, long curly brown hair, and golden-brown skin.

I cleared my throat and asked, "I am. And who are you?"

"My name is Aria, and Iris and I hang out quite a bit. What's up?" Her smile lit up her entire face.

I did my best to control the urge to raise an eyebrow at her because I didn't remember Iris mentioning anyone named Aria, but I wasn't in the position to argue. "Have you seen her around?"

Aria paused for a moment before she shook her head. "I think the last time I saw her had to be over a week ago. Is everything okay?"

"Yeah, it's fine." I shrugged, hoping to appear as calm as possible. "But if you see her, could you tell her to contact Bianca?"

"I can do that. I need to head to the library, but is there anything else I could do for you?"

I shook my head and said, "Thanks, I'll be right behind you."

With a slight nod, Aria walked away, and once again, I was alone. For some reason, I didn't trust her one bit, but if she was telling the truth, the last time Iris was seen might have been the evening of the Chevalier party.

And the only people I knew who were for sure at the party were Nash and Raven.

THROUGHOUT MY DRIVE back to my apartment, the only thing I could think about was the dreaded call I needed to make. My brother was one of the last people I wanted to speak to right now. After what I'd found out he'd done, forgiving him wasn't in the cards at the moment.

But talking to Raven wasn't out of the realm of possibilities.

Once I was in the privacy of my place and had thrown most of my things down on the counter, I grabbed my phone and quickly found Raven's number. I swallowed hard as I listened to the phone ring, but thankfully it only rang twice before she picked up.

"Hey, Bianca."

"Hi," I said nervously and hated myself for it. "Do you have a second to talk?"

"Sure. What's up?"

"You know that Chevalier party on Westwick's campus that happened about a week ago?" I was being awkward as hell, but at least it felt as if I was getting somewhere.

"Yeah. What about it?"

Silence hung between us for a moment while I tried to piece together my words. "Did you happen to see Iris there?"

Raven didn't speak for a moment, and I swore that I stopped breathing. Why did it feel as if it was taking her so long to respond to me?

"I did. Nash and I spoke with her for a bit."

Bingo. "Do you happen to remember if you saw her leave that night?"

"What's going on, Bianca?"

I sighed. "Please just answer my question."

"Um, the three of us were chatting, and then Soren Grant interrupted us. They danced together for a bit before they left the room, and that was the last I saw of her. Iris seemed fine."

I didn't know what to feel about the news. I'd gotten one step closer to finding out what happened to Iris, and I wasn't shocked to find that he'd been the one who had last been seen with her as of now. If he went through the trouble of sending her expensive electronics and became her substitute professor in order to stalk her more, what else was he capable of?

Fuck. I ran a hand through my hair as I tried to think of what to do next. My first instinct was to storm up to his house and demand to see Iris. But that was an even more ridiculous idea than the one I'd just had about going up to Westwick University with no plan.

"Hey, listen," Raven started before I could utter another word. "Nash would like to speak to you."

My throat became dry as a mix of anger and dread flowed through me. The last thing I needed, especially with this new information, was to deal with my brother and his attempts to "protect" me.

But I also couldn't hang up the phone right now with Raven in the room with him.

"Okay. I'll talk to him."

There was some shuffling in the background followed by a heavy silence, before I finally heard his voice. "Hey."

I barely contained the anger that was pulsing through me. The urge to snap at him was strong. "What do you want, Nash?"

"Is that how you greet me now?" His voice told me that he was taken aback about my attitude, and I didn't care.

"I'm not in the mood for being nice," I said. "What do you want to talk about?"

"You're acting like a child right now. What crawled up your ass and died?"

"The fact that my brother couldn't mind his own damn

business and had to get involved with my fucking love life, that's what."

"What are you talking about?"

"I'm talking about the deal you made with Easton."

That was when it clicked for him. "The only way you would know about that is if Easton told you. Since when did the two of you become best friends?"

His question unleashed the fury within me, and there was no stopping what came out of my mouth next. "When he started fucking me."

Nash's silence was deafening. The only thing I could hear was the sound of his breathing picking up. and I could tell he was getting angrier by the second.

Part of me wished I could take it back, but also, keeping this to myself had been an unexpected burden. This needed to get out there.

"Does Dad know about this, especially with your impending engagement?"

I wasn't surprised that Nash had been told about Dad's ultimatum. I was irritated that he was bringing it up in this manner, and I knew it was the result of him trying to get back at me for admitting that Easton and I had sex with each other.

"No, he doesn't, and to be honest, I don't care if he knows or not."

"Of course, you don't. If you did, none of this would have happened."

"Bullshit. You set your deal in motion before Easton and I slept together, so don't think you can remove the blame from yourself."

"I was just trying to protect you from him."

Nothing that was being said lessened my anger. In fact, him trying to justify it was doing nothing but upsetting me more.

"From what? You barely knew him at the time you put the deal into motion."

There was a pause from Nash before he spoke again. "There are some things you don't know about him that I do, Bianca."

"So going behind my back was the answer? No, fuck you and fuck him too!" I shouted just before I ended the call. I slammed my phone on the counter and stared at it. My heart felt as if it was slamming around my body, and my chest heaved to compensate for it. I blinked back the sting of tears that had more to do with anger and hurt than sadness.

Nash and I had been through so much together, and for us to have this colossal fight was heartbreaking. My best friend was missing, and my brother and I were fighting. Any hope I'd had of this being a good day was now tossed into the garbage.

I normally craved being alone, but this was the most alone I'd felt in my entire life. My parents were assholes who only cared about my father's political career, my brother had the nerve to try to dictate my dating life, and my best friend was missing.

Maybe things were better this way. Outside of my desire to find Iris, I wanted nothing more than to escape from the gilded cage I was trapped in. Maybe freedom was the answer.

I tried to hide my tears behind the fake smile on my face but failed. I tabled those thoughts as I couldn't fight against my tears now. They flowed from my face like a waterfall, with no end in sight. As my gaze wandered around the spacious apartment, it landed on one spot in particular.

I hated that my gaze drifted toward where I stored my alcohol. The desire to drown my sorrows in a drink of some kind was strong. I debated getting a drink, but I knew it was pointless because it wouldn't take this pain away.

Instead, I walked away, determined to come up with a plan that would get me out of this sham of an engagement and bring my best friend back home.

4

EASTON

I walked out of my philosophy class as the world's weight bore down on my shoulders. My thoughts about one person in particular consumed me, and before I could think twice about it, I found myself pulling out my phone and found the number I wanted. I couldn't deny that I was hoping to hear her voice and ease the tension that had been building up inside me. It didn't matter that she was pissed at me, as long as I got to hear her voice.

But she didn't answer.

My frustration grew with each ring, but at least she hadn't sent me to her voicemail.

"Damn it, Bianca," I muttered under my breath.

It probably wasn't the smartest idea to try to call Nash's sister right outside of the class that he and I shared together, but Nash had skipped class today. It was odd that he hadn't told me he wasn't coming today, and I wondered if it was because he knew about Bianca and me. But, if he did know, why wouldn't he have come to pay me a visit?

I didn't want to have to fight him, but, if it came down to

it, I would. Neither our families nor our coach and team would be pleased, but if that's the way he wanted to handle it, then so be it.

As I walked through campus to get to my car, I began to form a plan for how I could get back onto Bianca's good side, although I was questioning whether I deserved it or not.

As if someone had heard my thoughts, my phone vibrated in my hand, but it wasn't the Henson I was expecting. After debating with myself briefly, I answered the phone.

"Hey, Nash," I said as I tried to keep my tone even.

"Listen, I need you to come to Chevalier Manor tonight. We have something important we need to discuss."

The last thing I wanted to do was be in Nash's presence around a bunch of Chevaliers with this hanging over my head. However, it wasn't as if I could say no to the incoming chairman of this chapter.

"What time?"

"Nine p.m."

It would be good and dark by then, and I wondered if that was done by design. A prickly sensation flew across my neck as I thought about whether I should go there this evening.

"Fine," I said, resigned. "I'll be there."

"Good." Nash ended the call before I could say another word.

I was going to ask him if this was the reason why he hadn't made it to class today, but he hadn't given me the opportunity to do so. His curt attitude made me wonder if I was walking into a trap. Although this was just rumors at this point, it was thought that the rules were different once you stepped onto Chevalier property. I wasn't afraid of taking on Nash if necessary, but having to deal with other members of the secret society in addition to him hadn't been on my to-do list for today.

When I finally reached my SUV, I threw my book bag into the passenger seat as I slammed the driver's side door. The drive to my apartment was quiet because my mind was filled with nothing but thoughts of how to fix this shit.

If Bianca hadn't told her brother about what happened between us, I needed to come clean first. Nash would still be pissed, but it might serve me better to be the one to break the news to him. If he would give me a chance to explain why I did what I did and why I now wanted to make it up to her, then maybe this would go smoother. It seemed like wishful thinking, but that was where I was at this point.

When I arrived home, I distracted myself by working on some of the homework I desperately needed to do. On top of all of this, the last thing I needed to do was fuck up my grades, because I wasn't sure if I would recover even with the money my parents would be willing to throw in to convince the school to pass me.

When I took a break from studying, I stretched my body and reached for my phone. I quickly found the texting thread that Bianca and I shared and typed out a quick text to her.

> Me: I know you're pissed, but we need to talk. I will find a way to do so, one way or another.

Threatening her wasn't the best course of action, but I was determined to show her that I wouldn't give up, no matter what. I grabbed a meal that my mother had dropped off at my apartment a couple of days ago and ate that while I went back to my coursework.

Working on my homework and having dinner ate up most of the time I needed to burn until it was time for me to head over to Chevalier Manor. I took a shower, changed my clothes, and then left my apartment. As I put my SUV into drive, I couldn't help but wonder about the uneasy feeling that had settled into my stomach. I tried to brush it off as being on edge about everything since things had blown up between Bianca and me, but my gut was telling me I wasn't wrong. As I tightened my grip on the steering wheel, I tried to mentally prepare myself for any surprises that might be thrown my way as a result of my stepping foot onto their grounds.

The manor came into view, its sprawling stone walls stark against the night sky. When I pulled my vehicle into the Chevalier Manor driveway, an eerie feeling passed over me. Something about this felt all wrong. As I pulled to a stop, I noticed there was no one around.

I turned off the engine and stepped out of the vehicle. But I wasn't alone for long.

A hand grabbed me from behind, and a dark hood was thrown over my eyes. Panic and confusion warred inside me as I fought against whoever had a hold on me. Who the fuck was this? What did they want? I struggled against the hands restraining me, and I was able to put together that two men were holding me, but I couldn't break free.

As they began to drag me, I assumed toward Chevalier Manor, my heart pounded hard in my chest as I stumbled along.

"If you assholes don't let me go..." I said, as I fought to get free. No one said anything back. They hadn't taken the bait.

They hauled me over uneven ground as my sneakers

brushed against rocks and sticks on the ground. I noticed the change in the ground and noticed that I was placed on a more even surface, and the sounds around me became quieter. I assumed I'd been brought into the house. There was more dragging, but when we finally stopped, I was shoved roughly into a chair. My arms were pulled so that they were behind my back, and I felt a zip tie being put around my wrists. I strained against the binds, but they didn't budge.

A floorboard creaked behind me. I whipped my head around, straining to see through the hood, but there was nothing but darkness surrounding me.

"Comfortable?" The voice was low and mocking, but after the last couple of minutes, I didn't expect anything else.

I calmed my emotions before I spoke because I didn't want to show anything like that. "Nash, this is a bit much. Take the fucking hood off me."

There was a brief pause and then a long, bitter laugh. I heard some commotion and then a hand grabbed the hood and snatched it from my head. I blinked at the sudden light, squinting against the glare as my eyes tried to adjust.

Nash stood before me; his stance deceptively casual as he stuffed his hands in the pockets of his leather jacket. But the anger I saw in his eyes was loud and clear.

He knew.

My mouth went dry. "Nash, listen to me—"

"No. You're the reason all this shit is happening. You've proven that you're not a man of your word." He took a step forward, his gaze never wavering from me. "You're a liar. There's no way you should be able to become a member of the Chevaliers."

"I'm not even sure what you're accusing me of." That part

was true. I assumed it was because of the deal he and I struck about his sister, but hell, it could be something else at this point.

"You're not?" He stared at me for a moment before he turned to the others in the room. "If you'd excuse us?"

I watched as three other guys I vaguely knew left the room, leaving Nash and me alone. He waited a moment before he turned to face me once more.

"Are you going to tell me that you didn't touch my sister? Are you going to continue to fucking lie to my face?"

"Nash it wasn't like—"

My words died on my lips as Nash's fist connected with my face. Pain exploded across my cheek. My head snapped to the side as spots danced across the wall. The metallic taste of blood filled my mouth.

When I shook my head and looked up, I struggled to focus on Nash until he moved into my line of vision. Nash leaned over me, and the rage in his eyes was obvious. "Did you think I wouldn't find out?"

He drew back his fist again. I shifted as the zip ties dug into my wrists, but I screamed first. "If you really want to handle this one-on-one, we can fight it out."

"That would be fitting for you, wouldn't it? That way you might get the upper hand, right?"

Nash narrowed his eyes at me, and I wondered if he was thinking about what I said. I appealed to his ego on purpose because if he wanted to beat the shit out of me, he'd want to do it fair and square.

I watched as he took out a pocketknife from his coat pocket and cut the zip ties that were around my wrists. A rush of relief flooded my body as my hands were freed, but he still held the knife close to me, so I knew better than to think this was over.

Nash took a step back and gestured for me to stand up. I rose to my feet, mentally preparing for what was about to occur. We stared each other down, both of us ready for what was about to come.

The air between us grew thicker the longer we stood there, while neither of us dared to make the first move. Seemingly out of nowhere, Nash lunged at me with a powerful punch, but I managed to dodge it just in time, and that only seemed to piss him off more. His fists flew at me as fast as lightning, each one coming faster than the last. I did my best to dodge them and block my body from them whenever I could. I managed to get a few hits in as well, proud to be able to execute payback for him punching me in the face when he had the upper hand.

I attributed most of my reflexes to the adrenaline pumping through my veins and my training due to football, and I was grateful for that.

"Enough!"

I temporarily took my eyes off Nash and was relieved when he did the same. If he hadn't, he would have easily gotten a shot in because of me being distracted. I looked up and saw a man in a suit walking toward us. "This is ridiculous."

Nash immediately stopped and before he turned away from me, I could still see the rage in his eyes, but the hold this man had over him seemed to be stronger. "Chairman Townsend, you aren't supposed to be here until tomorrow."

"Glad I made it up here tonight to see you throw away everything you worked so hard for. Whatever you're fighting with him over isn't worth this. You're supposed to be a leader for this organization and leaders don't step this low. Now, you and I have to talk."

Nash paused for a beat before he turned to me and said, "Tomorrow evening, you'll receive a message about what time and the location of where you need to be if you wish to start your trials to see if you'll become a Chevalier. I won't go gentle on you because of your injuries either."

The shock I felt knowing I was still invited to anything related to the Chevaliers barely registered when I replied, "Good... because I wouldn't expect anything less."

5

EASTON

I glanced down at the piece of paper in my hand as I reread it for the millionth time wondering exactly what the fuck I was doing. Here I was, standing outside of a large, abandoned warehouse. I was slightly confused, but mostly intrigued about why I was here. This was the first task that would help prove why I should be a member of the Chevaliers. I had no idea what to expect, but the mystery and intrigue surrounding all of this and my run-in with Nash only fueled my determination.

What I did expect was for this challenge to be physical. For Nash to have said that he wasn't going to take it easy on me today because of any pain I might be feeling was a strong hint toward that. It was the reason why I made sure to take care of myself the best I could to physically prepare for whatever this would be.

I was still sore from the fight Nash, and I had the evening before, but I didn't care. I was even more determined to beat whatever challenge they threw at me. I walked up to what looked to be a wooden door and stepped inside.

At first, I was met with darkness and silence. The urge to pull out my phone and use it as a flashlight was strong, but I refrained. I wanted to show that I wasn't afraid of this task.

I didn't have long to wait.

Somewhere in the distance, a door creaked open. Then I heard footsteps, but they weren't coming toward me. My breath caught in my throat, but I didn't move. I refused to convey any emotion that might make anyone think I was afraid of whatever might happen tonight.

"Welcome to your first challenge, Easton Beaumont. Your objective is simple. You must pass through the gates of darkness and emerge into the light by completing your tasks. We've hidden an item important to our organization in this warehouse. There are a series of obstacles standing in the way of you getting close to and then finding it. Find the item and make it out."

"What is this, some sort of competition from a reality television show?"

No one responded to my inquiry, and I was left in silence. Instead of waiting for something else to happen, I walked further into the warehouse, and that's when the lights in the warehouse were turned on, but not to their full potential. While I wished the lights were turned on to their full capacity, any source of light would be helpful when it came to getting through this.

The first obstacle looked to be a bunch of pipes and beams suspended over a pit of who knows what. It looked to be some type of liquid, but what exactly it was, I didn't have the slightest clue. Next to a ladder, which I assumed I was supposed to climb up to start the course, was a set of gloves. Were these pipes even sturdy enough to hold my weight?

Fine. If that's how they wanted to play it, then so be it. I stuffed my hands in the gloves and sighed. I reached out to grab the ladder rung and started my ascension. When I made it to the top, I looked down, and that was probably the dumbest thing I could have done. With a deep breath, I reached for the first beam, and I swung my body to gain momentum so that I could make it to the next one.

My muscles ached as my body stretched into movements it shouldn't be, especially after the adventure it had been put through the previous evening. I could hear nothing due to my heart pounding in my ears, further forcing me to focus on what I needed to do to get through this hellhole.

Every swing was a battle, and nothing mattered but making it to the end without falling. When I emerged on the other side of this, my entire body was angry with me, and I couldn't blame it one bit. However, being able to achieve such a feat was pushing the adrenaline through me. Waiting for me was a key, and I wondered what it would open. As I took a moment to catch my breath, the fact that I still had more hurdles to face hit home.

I wouldn't be leaving here until I completed every challenge they set forth and beat this task. It took some time for me to complete every obstacle, but when I reached the end of the warehouse, I found a small box sitting on a pedestal. I used the key that I found and stuck it into the box and turned.

I didn't know what I'd been expecting, but when I found a gold coin in the box, I couldn't lie and say I wasn't surprised. It was then that the lights were turned up, and I covered my eyes as I felt almost blinded by the brightness.

Clapping erupted from all corners of the warehouse as I

glanced around, taking everything in. Guys that I recognized, and some that I didn't, came out of the shadows. I didn't realize how many people I knew were members of the organization.

I mouthed the word thank you and then grabbed my knees and looked down at the ground once more, until a pair of shoes came into my view.

"Congratulations, Easton," the voice said. "You have passed the first task, but now we must step things up a notch."

"What do you mean?"

"Why don't you climb down and find out? Walk over to the spot on the wall marked with an X."

I stood motionless for a moment before I did as I was told. I climbed down the metal ladder, and once I was on the ground, I walked over to the gold X on the wall. I found a bat leaning on the wall and I grabbed it, assuming it would come in handy. The open space I was now in made me wonder what was coming next. "What now?"

"Dodge the drones."

There was silence for a second before I heard a grinding sound. Dozens of drones whirred into view, and they looked like something out of a movie. They came in an assortment of shapes and sizes, and I wasn't sure which one to focus on first.

My heart pounded as they flew around the room. This was impossible. There was no way to get past them. To make matters worse, I couldn't tell what type of weapons they had, so I didn't know what their capabilities were when it came to hurting me.

But I couldn't back down. I steeled myself and took a deep breath. It was go time.

The drones descended in a flurry of movement and noise. I swung with the bat, grateful that before I focused on football, I'd played baseball too. I easily knocked away the smaller drones, but a larger one slammed into my side. I grunted in pain and shoved it out of the way, but I could hear that more were coming.

Fuck.

I needed to think because I had to outsmart them. Ducking under one drone, I managed to hit two of the others at the same time. Having a small break, I caught my breath and swung again and again. When I'd reached the final drone, I hit it with that bat and watched as it landed on the ground. I then stepped on the drone, enjoying the feeling of squishing it beneath my boot.

The voice spoke again and said, "Well done. Now it is time for round three. Walk through that door to the left."

I steadied my breathing before walking over and through the door. For a split second I could see before everything descended into pure darkness. The door slammed behind me, sealing me in.

Assholes. I strained my eyes but couldn't see anything, not even my hand in front of my face.

"The Dark Obstacle Course will test your senses and reflexes," the voice said. "You have ten minutes to reach the exit. If you do not make it in time... well, we wouldn't want to spoil the surprise. Begin."

Ten minutes. I gritted my teeth. I could do anything for ten minutes. Using my hands, I felt along the wall, slowly moving forward step by step. I tried to ignore the aching of my body, but it wasn't going well.

I cursed as I nearly fell headfirst into what seemed to be a pit. I walked around the edge of it. What other traps did they have planned?

Suddenly something hit me in the gut out of nowhere, and it took me a moment to recover in order to keep from crashing to the ground. I wasn't sure what it was, but I knew it was swinging back and forth. I needed to figure out its timing so that I could avoid getting hit again.

It took a little longer than planned, but soon I was on the other side of whatever was swinging toward me, and it had only clipped my leg.

Diving between the obstacles forced so much more physical exertion and having to deal with the fact that it was almost pitch black made things more difficult, but also forced me to rely on my other senses more. My body was exhausted and bruised, but I was determined to make it through.

My hand struck a wooden surface, and I found my saving grace: a doorway. I threw my body weight onto the door, and as it opened, the light blinded me. I had made it.

Breathless, I turned to the clock on the wall. I read the number that appeared on the television screen in front of me fifteen times before I believed it. Eight minutes and two seconds. I leaned against the wall to catch my breath, but I couldn't fight the grin that crossed my face. Tonight had been one big test, but I had prevailed.

I let out a deep breath. A sense of relief rushed through my body at having completed these challenges. While I knew this was only day one, and there would be more challenges I would need to face, it felt good to claim this win. I didn't know how much it would take to prove that I was worthy of being a Chevalier. I went back to trying to catch my breath as I waited for Nash to leave. But he didn't.

"Have you spoken to Bianca recently?"

My heart felt as if it stopped beating. The question forced me to jerk my head up to look at him given it was the reason we literally had a fist fight the day before. His gaze burned a hole into me even though he was the one that brought her up.

I shook my head. "Not recently. Why?"

The smirk that formed on his face told me all I needed to know regarding what he was about to say. It wasn't going to be anything good.

"Her engagement is going to be announced soon."

I think my soul left my body. What did he just say? There was no way that I heard him correctly. I stood up to my full height and said, "What did you just say?"

"Bianca is engaged. She's moving on from whatever you two did. You should do the same."

"You're full of shit."

Nash crossed his arms across his chest. "You don't have to believe me. There will be an announcement in a couple of days."

I glared at him and turned away, taking my time to shake the hands of several Chevaliers before I left the building. It wasn't the smartest thing to piss off the chairman of the organization that you're about to join, but I didn't care. I was raging inside and being able to maintain control of myself as I walked out of this warehouse was a miracle.

As I stepped into my SUV and closed the door, my emotions swirled inside me like a tornado. It took everything in me not to wipe the smirk off Nash's face.

Bianca was engaged.

There was no way that was possible.

I clenched the steering wheel, and it was only when I saw people leaving the warehouse that I snapped out of it. I threw my vehicle into reverse and backed up to give myself enough room to turn and head down the street to the main road. Nothing about any of this made any sense.

My thoughts didn't make any sense, and I was acting on pure instinct. There was no way I was going to just let this news fly.

I hadn't been willing to admit it to myself until this moment, although it had been true for a long time. Bianca was mine. I would turn everything in this universe to ashes to have her. And if I couldn't, I would make sure no one else would either.

6

BIANCA

I sighed as I rubbed a hand down my face. Between the hours I'd spent searching for Iris both online and in person and trying to figure out a way to get out of this stupid engagement, I was beat. The only thing I could find was a trail of breadcrumbs that seemingly led to nowhere.

I checked her social media accounts, hoping to find anything that would allude to where she could be. But there was nothing to find.

I'd been up to Westwick University several times since she went missing, in hopes of finding something, but those all turned up empty as well. In fact, that was where I was once again, trying to see if there was something I missed. I'd even run into Aria again and she still hadn't seen or heard from her. It was as if she had vanished into thin air.

The more I searched for her, the more my concern for her increased. There was no doubt in my mind that something was wrong. It was a feeling that had settled in my gut and refused to go away.

As I walked back to my car, having explored the

economics building on Westwick's campus, a chill ran through me like wildfire, quickly spreading throughout my whole body. It was starting to get dark, and being anywhere near Westwick when it was light outside was creepy enough, but being here as the sun was setting was even worse. I looked around to see if I saw anyone, but I didn't. With a renewed sense of focus, I put my head down and walked faster to my car. I couldn't shake off the feeling that someone was following me.

I wanted to tell myself that I was imagining things, but I didn't want to take the chance that I wasn't.

Once I reached my car, I locked my car doors and swallowed the lump in my throat. I attributed my skittish behavior to the fact that I was scared for Iris, and that I hated being anywhere near Westwick, let alone on its campus.

I started my car and pulled out of the parking lot without taking another look back at the place I'd just left. As I was driving back to my apartment, an idea popped into my head. I glanced down at my console and saw that it was getting kind of late, but if I didn't at least try this idea, it would haunt me until I did.

I pulled out my phone and mumbled the words I wanted to say into it. It found the phone number I asked it to call, and I waited for the call to connect.

"Hello? Bianca?"

"Hi, Gran," I said, using the name that Iris's grandmother told me to call her when we first met.

"How are you doing?"

"I'm good. Hey, I'm in my car and thought it would be a good time to visit you because I'm not too far from your house," I said, lying with ease. "Do you mind if I stop by to see you?"

"Of course. Why don't I whip up some dinner? It would be nice to have you over for dinner."

I thought it was a bit weird that she didn't ask if I was with Iris. "Sure, that sounds like a plan. I'm going to make a U-turn and I'll be there as soon as I can."

"Okay. I'll see you soon, dear."

I disconnected the call and pulled over to the side of the road. I quickly found the directions to Gran's home and waited for my car's GPS to process the new entry. Once it found the quickest route, I put my car into drive and pulled a U-turn to get on the road to Gran's.

When I arrived at Gran's home, I was feeling more anxious than I'd been at Westwick. What was I going to say? How much should I let her in on what I suspected was going on?

I parked my car and looked up at the front door. Gran was already standing at the door with a smile on her face. She was still wearing an apron that I assumed she put on to protect her clothes while cooking.

She gave me a warm hug and squeezed. Everything about her showed how much of a gentle, strong soul she was. Being in her presence reminded me of how long it had been since I'd seen her. When she pulled away, she gave me a genuine smile and said, "It is so nice to see you in person. What brings you here?"

As I stepped into the house, I felt a mixture of emotions, but I tried my best to focus on the woman in front of me. "Something told me to try to come visit you today, and I followed that gut feeling."

It wasn't a lie.

"I'm not going to complain about that. We're having homemade soup and bread. I hope that's okay."

I gave her a grin and said, "That sounds absolutely perfect."

We took a seat at the dining room table as the lovely smell from the soup lingered in the air, and Gran began to talk about Iris. She told me how she missed her granddaughter dearly and that she would be gone for the next few weeks while studying abroad.

"So the reason I wanted to come here was because I wanted to check on you."

"I appreciate it, dear. With Iris not being in the country right now, it's been lonely."

It took everything within me not to drop my spoon on the floor. I needed to choose my words wisely because I didn't want to alarm her in any way. "Have you spoken to her since she's been gone?"

Gran sighed and said, "We've emailed back and forth, but she hasn't called me back. I don't want to encroach on her study abroad trip of a lifetime, but I wish she'd call." Her voice trembled slightly before she continued. "At least she'll be home in a couple of weeks."

I was pretty sure that it wasn't Iris emailing Gran, and that thought made me feel sick to my stomach as well as want to rage. How could you do this to the woman in front of me who has already lost so much?

A frown covered Gran's face as her finger absentmindedly traced the rim of her soup bowl, a clear indication that she was thinking. I didn't say a word, choosing to continue to watch her. My heart ached because of the loneliness she must be feeling. I felt it on some level too.

"I miss her dearly, you know," she continued, a soft sigh escaping her lips. "The house felt so empty without her when she went away to college, and now it feels even more empty since I haven't been able to hear her voice."

"I know, Gran," I replied, reaching across the table to cover her hand with mine. "I miss her too."

"I keep telling myself that each day that passes means she's closer to coming back home. Have you heard from her at all?"

I felt bad for what I was about to say, but it wasn't worth dragging Gran into this. "I've gotten a couple of emails too. She asked me to come see you and to give you a hug for her."

I saw the tears well up in her eyes and I felt like trash. I could have gotten my point across without saying that.

She sniffed and wiped her eyes. "Well, that's very sweet of her. I love it when you two come to visit me."

I smiled, glad to have brought some joy into this moment. We continued to enjoy our dinner and talked about everything under the sun.

The conversation flowed effortlessly, touching on a little bit of everything. From the latest bestseller she was reading to some of the activities I was doing in my sorority. It was nice to have a lovely conversation where the other person didn't have ulterior motives.

"I can't believe how much the world has changed and how quickly technology is evolving," she mused, setting down her spoon to lean back in her chair. "Sometimes, it feels like I blinked, and everything just raced ahead."

I chuckled, picturing Gran racing against time. "Don't

worry, Gran. You're not that far behind," I teased. "After all, you're excellent at texting."

Gran chuckled and I was happy to have brought a smile back to her face. Although I was talking to her, I couldn't help but think that whoever had kidnapped Iris had put together an elaborate scheme to keep her location hidden.

With Soren, being the last one to see her alive, the chances were high that he'd done this. But why?

What I did know was that I needed to tread carefully.

While my visit to Gran's had been lovely, it had done little to answer any of the questions I had. There was so much more that I didn't know, but I was determined to investigate it further.

I knew it wouldn't be easy, and I had no idea who I was dealing with. However, with that thought in mind, I made a mental promise to Gran that I would find out what happened to her granddaughter. And I didn't care how long it took.

7

BIANCA

The bass thumped in my chest as I pushed through the crowd. I absolutely loved the feeling it shoved through my body. I was in my element, in a time where I could ignore my problems and embrace my wild side, although it was temporary. The warm, sweaty bodies that I touched would have been icky normally, but I was used to this. The jeans and black tank top that I'd chosen to wear under my winter coat had come in handy due to the humidity that was prevalent in this room. Making my way through the couples that were grinding on the dance floor wasn't my favorite sport, but it was what I needed to do to get to where I wanted to go.

Let's be honest. I wasn't the only college student here who was trying to outrun their problems using alcohol as a temporary Band-Aid.

I'd said goodbye to some of my sorority sisters that I'd come to the party with, and I wasn't staying much longer. In fact, I was going to get my coat from the back room that I'd tossed it in earlier that night.

The music faded away when I collided with someone. To their credit, they did their best to steady me so I didn't fall over. When my eyes met theirs, my mouth opened in shock.

Landon.

He was the person who kept me from falling and still had his hands on my arms. His touch was warm, and I wasn't sure how it made me feel. There was something about him that made me feel strange, but I couldn't quite place it.

I remember briefly meeting him at a party when I'd come here for a campus visit my senior year. It was also the same night Easton took my virginity.

"Bianca?" he asked, and I was surprised he managed to recall my name. A smile appeared on his face as his eyes scanned mine.

"It's been a while, Landon," I blurted out without thinking about it first.

Brentson was a big university, but even I was surprised that this was the first time I was running into him on campus. I hadn't really thought of him since the night we met, but I assumed he'd transferred or something.

Obviously, I was wrong.

"That it has. I didn't expect to see you here tonight. Do you have time to talk?"

I nodded in agreement. It had been the last thing I was expecting too.

We made our way to a quieter spot in order to get away from the blaring music and nosy eyes. Landon was a welcomed temporary distraction. If talking to him could soothe my overactive thoughts, I was willing to take it. Plus, it was probably better than drinking my sorrows away. We talked about our courses and how the school year was going so far, but we didn't delve into anything too personal. For a moment, I was able to push away thoughts of Easton and relish the comfort of a normal conversation.

However, that didn't last long.

As always, I found my thoughts circling back to Easton and comparing him to some of the things that Landon was saying. Every comment and laugh that I shared with Landon twisted my heart a bit more. I hated that this was what I'd become, but what could I do about it now?

"Hey, are you okay?" Landon asked, pulling me out of my thoughts. His expression was one of genuine concern, making me feel guilty about using him as a way to not think of Easton.

I nodded, forcing a smile on my face. "Just a little tired."

He didn't need to know about everything that was going on in my life because it wasn't any of his business, but I hated that I lied with such ease.

Although the energy around me hadn't changed, I had. My heart was no longer into partying with my thoughts returning to Easton even though I was talking to Landon. It honestly wasn't fair to either of them, but I couldn't stop my mind from doing it.

When I checked the time on my phone, I noticed that it was one in the morning, reminding me that I had been on my way out of here when Landon stopped me. I really needed to head home.

"I should probably go. It's getting pretty late."

"Do you want me to take you home?"

I stared at him for a moment and shook my head, deciding I didn't want to take him away from the party if he was having fun. "It's okay. I'll call a car to get me."

"Okay. Then I'll see you around."

Landon left without another word, and I was left watching him walk away, wondering when I would see him again.

I used my phone to call a car and as I made my way outside, I saw the bright headlights of a vehicle slowing down to a stop near the house I'd been partying at. After taking a few deep breaths, I opened the door of the car I ordered and got inside. As the car drove me home, I thought about how strange it was to see Landon again after so long.

When I finally made it back home, all I wanted to do was take a shower and try to clear my head. I walked into my bathroom and turned on the showerhead. I let the hot water run over me as images and thoughts rushed through my mind. It felt like an eternity before I finally stepped out of the shower and wrapped myself up in a towel.

As much as I wanted to go straight to bed, my body was dying for something to snack on. So instead of stopping in my bedroom, I went into the kitchen and opened up the fridge. I found a container of leftover butter chicken and popped it into the microwave. I also snagged a glass of water while I waited for my food to reheat. Once it had finished heating up, I pulled out the container and grabbed a fork before sitting down at the kitchen counter to eat.

The food was delicious and hit the spot. I probably shouldn't be eating something this heavy so late at night, but it was the perfect food to satisfy me right now.

When I was done, I pushed away my unfinished plate of food before standing up from the bar. It was time for me to wash these up and to get ready for bed.

I quickly cleaned my dishes, because the sooner I did so,

the sooner I could get to bed. I had to admit, washing dishes tonight was therapeutic in a way, because some of the stress and worry that I had flowed down the drain along with the soap and the suds. When I was done, I walked to my bedroom and changed into a pair of comfortable pajamas. Afterward, I crawled into bed, and I sighed as I pulled up the sheet and blankets to cover myself.

My head was spinning from all that had happened. Being in the safety of my own home gave me a sense of peace that I hadn't felt since before this whole mess began. I closed my eyes, in hopes that my exhaustion would kick in and I would soon be in a restful sleep.

I hated this.

I was still awake after tossing and turning most of the night over my encounter with Landon. I really needed to get to sleep. For some reason, I couldn't turn my brain off, so I was stuck trying to find a comfortable position until my mind decided to give me a reprieve.

An idea popped into my head that might give me the ability to stop thinking of the million and one things that seemed to crowd my mind on a regular basis.

I moved the long shirt I'd worn to bed out of my way so that my fingertips could touch my panties. I shifted the offending item out of the way and found myself wet. Maybe this was a great idea after all.

I ran a finger up and down my slit, choosing to let myself be my own lubrication, before rubbing it across my clit. I repeated the motion until a steady rhythm grew. With the way I was going, there was a chance that I wouldn't last long.

And then an image of Easton flashed in my mind. Yes, I

was still pissed at him, but the memory of what he'd done to my body was enough to send sparks straight to my pussy.

"Mmm," I said as I began to rub faster, wishing that his hands were on me instead of my own. My back arched as I found the spot I was looking for.

The memory of his hands on my skin made me shiver with need. Memories of how he fucked me in his SUV when no one had been around, swam to the surface. It would have been so easy for us to get caught, and the thrill of that had me coming harder than I'd ever come in my life. I wished he was here, but he was also the last person on Earth that I would want to see right now.

A moan followed as I grew closer to my goal. I could swear that I heard my heart pounding in my ears, and I loved every second of it.

With a sharp cry, my orgasm crashed over me in waves that I couldn't control. My body shook due to the force of it, and I rode out the dizzying high, prolonging it as long as I could.

My body felt wonderful after pleasuring myself, but there was still a sense of longing for him that I couldn't escape.

8

BIANCA

I sank deeper into the cushions of my couch as my mind raced back and forth with thoughts about how convoluted my world had become. My leg jittered angrily as I stared at what had to be over forty dresses which my mother had sent over for me to try on until I found one that would be appropriate to attend some holiday party engagements that I assumed Tristan Whitmore would be attending too. All it did was make me angry about this fake engagement all over again, and I wanted to take my time shredding each and every dress to soothe my feelings.

So far, there hadn't been any word about the photos leaking, but I felt as if every day, I was waiting for the other shoe to drop when it came to them. I was convinced it was only a matter of time before they did, and then we would be in major crises mode.

Just then, a notification sounded on my phone, interrupting my thoughts. It was the front desk, contacting me through their app, asking if I wanted them to let an Easton Beaumont up to my apartment. My heart freaked the fuck out as I read his name over and over again. I didn't want to believe that he was here, but I knew that security was tight, and they'd have verified it was Easton standing in the lobby.

I released a frustrated sigh before I typed out a response.

> Me: Yes, let him up. Thank you.

My phone landed with a thump on my counter as my anger won. The knot that was already sitting in my stomach tightened as I realized how silly it was for me to allow him to come up here, yet for some reason, I couldn't refuse his request. I wanted to see him.

I stood up and glanced around the room, and while it wasn't a complete mess, it could be neater, but I didn't have time nor the capacity to even try to do something about it. After all, I shouldn't be trying to make Easton comfortable because he'd had enough audacity to show up here unannounced.

Each second that passed was nothing but more time for my anger and anxiety to rise and take hold of me.

This was it.

The moment where I'd finally be able to confront Easton about him leaking the pictures he promised he wouldn't leak if I did as he asked. He was an asshole and a liar, and I needed to remember that.

I paced while I waited, needing something to do as I waited for the knock to sound through the door.

When it finally came, I brushed my hands down my thighs and took a deep breath. When I opened the door, Easton's green eyes greeted me and seemed to pierce through me.

There was nothing remorseful in his gaze, and he was anything but happy.

He barged into my apartment without saying a word, and I couldn't help but take in his appearance. Easton looked as if he'd been through hell and back. His hair was a tangled mess, and his clothes were disheveled. He was sporting a bruise on his cheek, and I wondered if he'd just gotten into a fight. He didn't appear to be drunk or high, though judging by his current appearance, I wouldn't have been surprised if he was.

Part of me wanted to ask what had happened, but it was none of my business. The most important thing was to get him out of here as quickly as possible.

"Why are you here?" I said as I closed the door, not wanting to draw the attention of any of my neighbors. "I didn't invite you to my home."

Easton didn't say a word as he walked over to my window overlooking Brentson's landscape. Apparently, it had captured his attention more than the issue at hand.

Sighing, I decided that I would have to push ahead with the issue because this conversation needed to happen whether he liked it or not. "What the hell are you doing here, Easton?"

He whipped around to face me, his eyes filled with fury, but there was something else there. Something I couldn't quite point out. "Are you fucking engaged?"

I did a double take at his words, somewhat shocked at the words that had come out of his mouth. I'd been mentally preparing myself to bring up the photos, not talk about the plan my parents decided would be the best way to combat any negative press that would come about as a result of these photos being made public. I took a step back and crossed my arms over my chest, bracing myself for his reaction before I responded to his question.

"My relationship status isn't any of your business."

"The hell it's not."

In the blink of an eye, he was standing in front of me, his lips crashing into mine. For a second, I kissed him back, before I came to my senses. I shoved him away and then slapped him, prepared to do more violence to him if necessary. Part of my reaction was because of what he'd done but I was also taking the anger I felt toward myself out on him. I shouldn't have fallen so easily back into his arms, especially given what I knew now.

I shouldn't have touched him, but my anger won out in this moment.

"How dare you?" My voice trembled with rage for the man in front of me.

"You don't have any feelings for him."

I didn't want to debate something that was obviously fake, but I needed to because Easton was overstepping so many boundaries.

"Fuck you. None of this is any of your business."

If Easton hadn't been angry when he entered my apartment, he definitely was now. I couldn't recall a time when I'd seen him this pissed off and all of it was focused on me.

"I'm making it my business, princess."

"Just like you made it your business to send those photos to my father?" There. I'd said it.

The fury in his eyes eased for a moment as he processed what I said. "I didn't—"

"Don't lie to me because I've seen them. I know the truth."

My voice shook with anger and while I wished it didn't, it wasn't going to stop me from saying what needed to be said. "You promised you wouldn't leak them, so in reality, all of this is your damn fault."

I glared at him as my arms tightened around my body. It finally felt like I slightly had the upper hand now. "You lied to me," I uttered each word slowly to make sure he knew how serious I was about this.

I didn't bother giving him an opportunity to speak. I tried to control the level of my voice, but I could hear it rising with every word. "You broke your promise, and now my parents want to make me marry Tristan Whitmore because of what he owns and who he knows that they believe would stop these photos from ruining my father's career. So yes, this bullshit is all your fault!"

"I swear I didn't send those photos to your father."

"Then how did he get them?"

Easton didn't respond this time. Instead, he studied me, and I wished I could peer inside of his mind to catch a glimpse of what he was thinking.

"Fucking answer me!" I screamed.

But of course, he didn't. Deep down, I wanted to believe him, but I knew that would be foolish.

"Since you won't answer that, tell me why you came here tonight," I said, all the while hating myself for wanting to know.

"Because I couldn't stay away."

Easton's words slashed through me like a sword. I was surprised that he admitted it. "Even though you'd just heard I was engaged?"

"Especially because you're engaged," he said, his voice

rough with emotion. "Nash's words cut through me as if they were a sword, and I know this is not what you really want."

"You don't know anything about me at this point."

"I know that you want to explore what you and I shared. You want to see where it goes. We can find a way to make it so that you won't have to marry Tristan."

A small light appeared at the end of the proverbial tunnel, but I knew it was too good to be true. This was all too much, and I was still pissed at him. Hell, I'd just slapped him one a few minutes ago.

"Easton, I can't do this," I whispered as I shook my head. "None of this is okay."

"What isn't okay about any of this?" He walked toward me until his face was only inches from mine once more. "We both know that you don't want to be engaged to Tristan."

"I don't want this," I mumbled to myself, or so I thought.

"What do you want?"

I bit the corner of my lip and looked him in the eye before I said, "I want you to leave."

"Is that what you really want?" he asked, his voice lowering to meet the same tone as mine.

"Yes," I said, my hands shaking. "I don't want to make a big show of it and have to call security or the police."

He shrugged in return. "Fine then. Goodbye, Bianca," he said, before slamming the door behind him.

I stood there for what felt like an eternity, staring at the closed door as I heard his heavy footsteps echo down the hallway until they faded away. I swallowed hard and walked back over to my couch with my bottom lip quivering. In the next second, I'd collapsed on the cushions. I took in several deep breaths to try to calm myself down, but I couldn't. The weight from everything was too much, and although I was caught off guard by this whole experience, I thought I held myself together well.

Plus, my first reaction hadn't been to grab a glass of wine, and for that I needed to count it as a win.

But that didn't remove the weight I felt pressing down on me over all this. When I tried to make the right move and do the right thing when it came to this or Iris's disappearance, it felt as if I was taking one step forward and two steps back. The hold this had on me was almost suffocating.

Closing my eyes, I slammed the door on the world around me and leaned my head back against the couch in order to allow my brain to just wander. That seemed to be the only thing that eased the tension I was feeling if I wasn't going to take a shot.

I opened my eyes and ran my fingers through my hair, trying to clear my thoughts. My heart was heavy with regret, but I'd been left with no other choice.

After getting antsy, I stood up from the couch and walked over to the window and took my time looking out at the twinkling lights of Brentson. There was so much beauty here, but also so much hate. And now I felt as if it was only a matter of time before all the hatred on the outside would be turned on me.

"Stop," I said to myself. "You are doing what you need to do."

But the pressure was still there.

I shook my head as I tried to shake the negative vibes that had entered. I needed to focus on how I was going to find Iris and get out of this engagement. Then I could figure out how I could make my life better.

However, deep down, I already knew I had the starting blocks for what would eventually bring peace to my life.

I needed to start living for me instead of trying to please everyone around me.

The realization slapped me in the face like a ton of bricks and I sighed. It would be much harder than just acknowledging it, but I needed to work toward it.

It was a matter of figuring out how. Because once I did, it would be time to rewrite my life and not let any of my past mistakes define me.

9

BIANCA

I took a sip from my glass of water before my fingers landed on my mousepad once more. I should have cleared my desk of the papers and notebooks before I decided to get to work on my laptop, but I hadn't. I was sitting at my desk, staring at the computer screen as I opened a new tab. After typing a URL and clicking a few buttons, I sat back and waited for the website to populate on my computer screen.

The idea for this came to me last night when I couldn't sleep. I was lying in bed, going through everything that had happened for the one thousandth time, and knew that if I couldn't fall asleep, I needed to be formulating a plan to get out of this engagement and potential marriage.

That's when it hit me.

If I wasn't here, I couldn't get married.

I paused for a moment to look out my window, allowing myself to get distracted momentarily before I took a deep breath. I turned my attention back to the website and searched until I found the virtual form I was looking for.

After spending most of the night wondering what I was going to do about this impending engagement, this morning, I took the first step by applying to open a new account at another bank.

My fingers trembled as I typed in the information. It felt as if I was sneaking around, which I was, but also, I was an adult and had every right to open a bank account if I wanted to. I didn't know if I would even be approved, given that I was a student and I didn't have my parents on the account, but it was worth a shot.

Then, if I could take small amounts of money out of my main bank account and deposit it into this account, maybe I could accumulate enough money to get the hell out of here. But I had no choice. I needed to escape this hell.

As I clicked "submit" on the application, my thoughts drifted back to Easton and what happened before he stormed out of my apartment the night before. I'd spent most of the night wondering if I believed that he didn't sell me out to my father.

Just after I closed the tab, I heard a knock at the door. My heart skipped a beat. Who could it be? There were very few people who could come in here without having the front desk reach out to tell me I had a visitor, and I didn't want to see any of them. I hesitated for a moment before making my way to the door.

"Who is it?" I asked as I dreaded the response I was about to receive.

"It's Nash."

What the fuck is he doing here?

Before I could second-guess myself, I opened the door to find Nash standing there. I stared at him for a moment and noticed how he looked the exact opposite of Easton yesterday. My eyes landed on his slightly bruised hand, briefly wondering if he'd had an incident related to football.

"Can I come in?" he asked.

I thought about it for a moment before nodding and stepping aside to let him in. As soon as he entered, I could feel the tension in the air, and I hated that we'd gotten to this place. The silence that passed between us was awkward. The only time I had memories of instances like this between Nash and I were when Mom would force us to apologize to one another when we were fighting. However, this was very different.

"What are you doing here, Nash?"

"I wanted to come over to see how you were."

I raised an eyebrow at him. A phone call or a text would have accomplished this without him having to go out of his way. I was willing to admit that we'd been close before all of this blew up, but I wasn't sure if I ever remember Nash stopping by to see how I was before.

"Is that the only reason?" I asked, my voice was icy to even my ear.

He paused for a moment before he spoke again. "No, I wanted to apologize for what happened with me telling Easton not to date you. I'd heard some things about Easton at the time and didn't want you to be someone added to his roster. The way I went about it was completely wrong, and I should have just spoken to you about what I'd heard."

I nodded slowly as I tried my best to remain composed despite every emotion that was swirling inside of me.

"I appreciate the fact that you came over here to tell me to my face." I waited a moment before I continued. "The last few days have been hell, and I'm still coming to terms with it all."

I appreciated my brother coming to me to apologize, but I thought about the plan I was beginning to implement that would get me out of this. I thought it best not to tell Nash anything about my plans to get the hell out of town.

It then dawned on me that I was prepared to do something similar to what his girlfriend had done years ago. If I did carry through with all of this, I couldn't leave Nash completely in the dark.

"It was the least I could do."

That sparked an idea in my brain. "I'm not thrilled with you even after the apology, but there's something you can do to make it up to me."

"What's that?"

"I need to find out where Iris is, and I think you might have been one of the last people to see her before she disappeared."

"Disappeared?"

I proceeded to explain to Nash all the events that happened since the night of the Chevalier party on Westwick University's campus. "I haven't talked to her since then. Raven mentioned that you both saw Iris with Soren Grant at the party."

A look crossed Nash's face but even though I'd known him all my life, I had no idea what he was thinking. What the hell was I missing between Iris, Soren, and the Chevaliers? "Wait a minute. Are you assuming that Iris's disappearance has something to do with the organization you'll be leading next semester?"

When Nash didn't answer, I thought I was going to jump

out of my skin. If Iris's disappearance had anything to do with the Chevaliers, this was an even bigger problem than I previously thought.

Getting Iris back was my overall goal, but now I knew I really had to tread carefully. From what I'd heard through the years from my grandfather and father, I didn't want to risk pissing them off because I knew the likelihood of me and Iris ending up dead was high.

"I need to know where Iris is and if she's okay, Nash."

"I know." He glanced around my living room before he sighed. "Things are a bit busy with Chevalier stuff and Eas—"

He stopped speaking and clenched his jaw as his eyes widened slightly. It was then I pieced together that he'd made a mistake. He'd almost said Easton's name in relation to the Chevaliers, right? Or was I misinterpreting this?

"What were you saying?" I decided to play it cool for now.

"I'll see what I can do, but if Soren's involved, I'm not sure how good things could be." There was a slight hesitation in his voice that made me wonder how much he might be able to accomplish.

"Don't say things like that, Nash." I needed to keep a level of positivity because it already felt as if everything around me was crashing and burning.

He opened his arms, and it was then that I realized I couldn't remember the last time I hugged my brother. Sure, we'd done it as kids, but the older we'd gotten, the more we pulled away from the habits we'd created as children.

"Okay," I said as I stepped into the hug.

It didn't last too long before Nash pulled away, and he gave me a small wave and walked out of my apartment. I turned on my heel, feeling slightly lighter than I'd felt before

Nash's visit. This was just the beginning of solving our issues, but I'd take it.

My mind was still on the conversation I'd just had with Nash as I walked over to my phone so that I could check my emails. Sure enough, there was a notification from the bank about my application to open a new account. My nerves were shot as I clicked and then scanned the email, quickly confirming that it was the standard "we've received your application" email.

At least they hadn't rejected me outright.

I packed my bag so I could leave and head to campus for the day. Maybe opening this account could serve as a way to also help Iris out. Finding her wouldn't be easy with the Chevaliers involved. And I might be forced to make a choice that I didn't want to make.

SPENDING QUITE a bit of time on campus had given me the ability to get my schoolwork done as well as think about some of the next steps I wanted to take. My plan wasn't fully formed, but pieces were starting to fall into place. At least the beginnings of something were being created. Now that I was back in my apartment, I could stare out the window without any judgment. The sky was painted in hues of orange and pink, but my mind was clouded with doubts and uncertainty. But I did know that taking even small steps toward something that resembled freedom was helping my mental health.

I kept thinking about the possibility of Soren kidnapping Iris, and how he was connected to the Chevaliers in some capacity.

I hadn't heard anything from Nash, and I couldn't help but wonder if it was because he hadn't heard anything on his end yet, or if he wasn't going to give me an update because he couldn't. I wouldn't be surprised if he chose the Chevaliers over me because that was what I was conditioned to believe as I'd seen my father do the same thing my entire life.

But what I hadn't expected was that Easton might be going through recruitment for the Chevaliers. If he was a part of this, I wasn't sure how much he actually knew, but it might not be a bad idea to have him on my side to help me find Iris. Plus, his family might have connections outside of the Chevaliers that he might be willing to let me use.

After all, he owed me, whether he leaked the photos or not. Heck, maybe he would be hell-bent on finding out who leaked the photos so he could clear his name.

Maybe getting close to Easton again under the guise of using him to get what I want wasn't such a bad idea. But I needed to keep my objective in mind.

I picked up my phone that I'd put face down on the cushion next to me when I sat down. I quickly typed out a message to Easton, read it over, and then pressed send.

It was a risky move for sure, but I had a feeling it might be one of the only ways to get to the bottom of this mess.

10

BIANCA

I hesitated slightly before I took a deep breath. I hated that I could only prolong this for so long. The only way to do this was to force myself to walk toward the coffee shop where Easton and I agreed to meet after I texted him yesterday evening. I shivered slightly when I exhaled and watched my breath leave my lips. It was a chilly day in Brentson, with the forecast calling for snow this evening. The quicker I got out of the cold air, the better.

This would be a pretty short meeting about the psychology project that we needed to wrap up soon. As I rushed into Beyond The Page, I thought about how I didn't want to get caught out in any bad weather if I could avoid it. The first thing that greeted me was the smell of freshly brewed coffee, and I couldn't wait to get a cup.

My eyes danced around the shop until I spotted Easton sitting at a small table by the window. It took him a moment, but he looked up when he saw me walking toward him. I somehow made my body continue moving without hesitation when his eyes met mine. The neutral expression that masked my thoughts about being in his presence once more was firmly set upon my face. The poker face I'd strengthened over the years of having to live in the public eye had come in handy this evening.

"Hey," he said, standing up to greet me.

"Hi," I said in return. I tried my best to sound casual, but I wasn't sure if I was giving a convincing performance. "Thanks for meeting me."

"Of course. How are you doing?"

I took a seat across from him and shrugged. "As well as can be expected, I suppose. You?"

"Same," he grunted while running a hand through his hair. "Listen, Bianca, about what happened—"

"This isn't what we are supposed to be talking about right now," I interrupted. "We're here to work on our psychology project, remember?"

There were other things I wanted to talk about too, but I wanted to do it in a more casual way. This wasn't the right time to ask him about the Chevaliers and what he might know.

"I think, after today, there shouldn't be much more we need to talk about outside of collaborating on the final presentation."

Thank goodness for that.

We ordered our drinks and continued to discuss the project, bouncing ideas off each other and taking notes based on what we'd come up with. Our focus on the project masked the tension that was simmering beneath the surface. But every once in a while, my eyes would meet his green ones, a silent dance that expressed so much of what we wanted to say out loud but couldn't.

I checked my watch and realized I had about ten minutes left before I needed to leave and still hopefully avoid the storm. I needed to make my move and shift the conversation quickly. When there was a lull in our conversation about the project, I leaned forward in hopes of trying to keep my voice down so no one around us could hear what we were saying.

"So I heard you are trying to become a Chevalier."

Easton's eyes snapped up to me in a flash, and I could see the surprise and disbelief in them. I hadn't been a hundred percent sure about the meaning behind the small slip Nash had made when he spoke to me the day before, but now, I was positive. This might all work in my favor.

"What did you hear?" he asked as if he was being careful with the words he was choosing to say.

I, too, concentrated on my next words because I didn't want to make a mistake. "Nothing much. Just that."

"I'm not supposed to be talking about any of this with you," he said firmly.

Excellent. The taste of this small victory was more than sweet. While Easton spoke, oblivious to the mistake he'd made, I fought to hold back my grin. His subtle confirmation was more than enough.

"Why? Why now? I assume you had the opportunity to join your freshman and sophomore year."

"I didn't actually."

That was strange for multiple reasons, including his connection to Nash, but also his family's status. I couldn't help but wonder why now?

However, none of that mattered. What mattered was what he could potentially do to help me find Iris.

"Why are you wondering about my involvement with the Chevaliers, Bianca?"

I leaned back in my chair and picked up the pen I'd been using to write notes about our project. I rolled the pen once and then twice between my fingers before I answered.

"I think there's something you might be able to help me with in exchange for leaking the photos of me."

There. I said it.

"I didn't leak any photos, and I'm going to prove that I didn't."

I shrugged. "Regardless, you're going to help me with this."

This time, Easton's gaze narrowed at me. "What makes you so sure of that?"

If I was being honest with myself, I wasn't sure. However, I wasn't about to let him in on that. "Because you want to make it up to me for the deal you struck with Nash." I leaned in again and lowered my voice. "You also want the opportunity to fuck me again."

When he didn't say anything right away, I knew my point had landed well.

"What do you need help with?"

"I need help finding out more information about the disappearance of my best friend. I think someone in the Chevaliers might be involved. Now, whether it's directly related to the organization, I'm not sure."

"And you aren't asking your brother?"

"I mentioned it to him, but I'm also not sure how much he's at liberty to tell me with him coming into a leadership role at Brentson in mere weeks."

"I understand that, but I need more information. What exactly happened to Iris? And what do you want me to do?"

"You know, I didn't even realize you knew her name."

Easton shrugged. "I know things about you, Bianca. Now answer my questions."

I told him about the last time I'd seen her, and that she hadn't been seen since the party at the Chevalier Manor on Westwick University's campus.

I cleared my throat and continued, "Having someone on the inside with access to the Chevaliers would be helpful for finding out what is going on, if she's alright, and how we can get her back. It has been a couple of weeks now that she's been missing, and we still don't have any leads or information on what happened to her."

"What do the Chevaliers have to do with this? Are you sure she didn't leave the party before her disappearance?"

I then told him about how Raven and Nash had seen her leave the main area with Soren Grant. I didn't know exactly what position he held in the organization, but I knew he was involved because my father had mentioned it in passing a while back.

"We spoke about him at the Cross family gala, right?"

I'd momentarily forgotten that Easton had been there and how annoyed I was that he'd attended with my family.

"Yes, and he lives somewhat close to Westwick. If he was the one who kidnapped her and took her there, then..."

"Why don't we just go up to his house and ask?"

My eyes widened at his idea. There was no way he'd just said that. "We cannot just go up to his house and ask about Iris. Hell, why not call the police while you're at it?"

"The last thing I would do is go to the police, especially

given how deep I'm in this." He sighed and ran a hand through his hair. "I could see what I can find out about Iris. Not sure how much I'd be told given that I'm not an initiated member yet, but I can see what I can do. Keep in mind, I also need to be careful because crossing the Chevaliers is well..."

He didn't need to say anything more because I knew what he meant. "Okay, just as long as you're willing to help."

"And I get what you offered in return."

The temperature increased in my body. I wanted to say something slick back, but the prospect of having sex with Easton again had scrambled my brain. I hated that he had this hold over me, but I couldn't deny the desire I had to have him fuck me again.

"And you don't mind the fact another man is in talks to propose to me?" There was no way he would still be okay with this arrangement if I had another man's ring on my finger.

"Nope."

There is no way he was being serious. "Or that deep down I hate you?" I stood up when it became painfully obvious that it was time for me to go.

I threw my coat on and zipped it up, waiting for Easton to speak again. When I looked up, he was staring at me.

There was something haunted in his stare that I couldn't exactly name. "Not in the slightest. Hate fucking was how we started up again anyway."

His words made me feel as if my heart was being tossed in my body. Of course, memories from our times together flashed in my mind. Instead, I turned my attention to the window of the coffee shop and saw that it hadn't started snowing. I told myself I was going to leave a while ago, and yet I was still here. I packed my bag, all the while ignoring Easton.

"I'll see you in class."

He said it as if it was a fact. I couldn't help but think of the bank account that I'd just gotten approved for. I turned to look at him as I slung my bag over my shoulder.

My fingers trembled as I dug into my bag to pull out a twenty because we hadn't decided who would be paying for this outing, and I was technically the one who invited Easton here.

However, Easton put his hand up. "I'm paying for our drinks."

I nodded as I saw him get ready to move. "Okay. Bye." I blurted the words out to avoid saying something awkward.

I left before he could get up and try to walk me to my car. The last thing I wanted to deal with was spending another second alone with him even though we were in public.

Once I was safely inside of my car, I locked the door behind me and let out the breath I'd been holding in. I hadn't realized how tense I'd been while I was in Easton's presence.

Could it have been the anger I still felt toward him? Potentially.

Could it be that I was now depending on him to work an angle for me when it came to Iris's disappearance? Possibly.

But it was definitely the fact that I would end up in his bed at some point soon in exchange for all of this.

Just before I put my car into drive, my phone buzzed from my purse seconds before the text message appeared on my dashboard.

I gasped at the message that appeared on the screen.

11

BIANCA

Staring at the screen of my dashboard, I reread the stark message on the screen. It wasn't a surprise to me that he'd gotten my number, but it didn't remove any of the shock from my system.

> Unknown Number: Hi Bianca, it's Tristan Whitmore. I wanted to grab dinner with you sometime this week.

The message had left me dumbfounded as desperation and panic flowed through me. If this engagement and marriage was supposed to happen, it made sense that we would have to actually see and interact with one another. But this wasn't something I could focus on right now. If I stayed out here any longer and Easton noticed, he'd be over here in a heartbeat.

I pulled out of my parking spot and drove toward my apartment. As I pulled into my parking space, small flurries had just begun to land on my windshield. I'd made it back to my place just in time.

As I grabbed my bag so that I could exit my vehicle, I felt it vibrate and knew I more than likely had another message. That one could wait too because there was no way I was dealing with this while I was outside, and it was snowing.

I entered my apartment and picked up my phone, and just as I was about to read what I assumed was Tristan's message, the device vibrated again. If he'd sent me three messages in less than fifteen minutes before I'd had the chance to respond, I was more than likely going to ignore him even more.

I sighed when I realized it was from my mother.

> Mom: Tristan should be reaching out to you soon. Remember to be nice and don't embarrass us. If he invites you out somewhere you're going and I'll send the team over to your apartment to help you get ready whenever it is.

I blew out an exasperated breath and rolled my eyes so hard I gave myself a headache. If I wasn't stuck in the middle of this, I would have laughed out loud.

I shifted through my texts until I came to the ones that were from an unknown number. Thankfully, this time it wasn't from my stalker, but I made sure to double check the numbers to see if my stalker and Tristan were one in the same. They weren't.

> Unknown Number: Do you have a preference?

Now I was left with a dilemma. Do I continue going through with this or say screw what my family says and run now?

I didn't have the means to run right now and get away without leaving a trail. I needed to play this smart. Plus, finding out about Iris's well-being was of utmost importance, and what was the likelihood of me being told that information if I was on the run?

I knew I needed to respond, but I wasn't sure how to. I'd never been in this situation before and everything within me didn't want to lead him on, but I also didn't want to anger him.

And how would my arrangement with Easton work with all of this?

Whatever, I'd deal with that when I needed to deal with it.

I ignored my mother's message, but I added Tristan's number to my phone and reread his message so I could compose a response.

> Me: I love Italian. What time were you thinking?

> Tristan: How about La Trattoria? I'll pick you up at 7:30 on Friday. The weather should be clear by then.

Holy shit. My heart raced as I processed what he said. La Trattoria was one of the newest restaurants in town and was hard to get reservations to. I didn't really want him to pick me up from my apartment because if I drove my own car, I could have my own way of getting back.

Then again, I had access to car services, but it would make things a bit more difficult because I'd have to wait, and I didn't know this man at all. Better to be safe than sorry, and it would also give me an excuse not to drink. Being out with him, I'm sure we'd be offered alcohol even though I was underage, and it wasn't something I wanted to risk.

Even if the urge to drink was staring me in the face right now in the privacy of my own apartment.

> Me: I will meet you there in time for the reservation.

That was final, leaving no room for him to argue with me. *Fuck it.*

I gave up on fighting the temptation and walked into my kitchen to get a glass of wine. I tore the cork out of the bottle with my teeth. It took me mere seconds to get the wine into a glass and bring it to my lips.

As I was sipping my wine, I couldn't help but wonder what Tristan got out of all of this. From what I'd seen, I couldn't imagine Tristan having an issue with dating, so what did he get by being in a fake engagement and potentially married to me?

Speaking of, my phone vibrated once more, and I saw that it was from him.

> Tristan: Okay, see you then.

Crisis averted.

But there was still one issue I needed to deal with.

I didn't feel the need to say another word to Tristan, but I did start typing a message to my mother.

Me: Dinner with Tristan is this Friday, weather permitting. Do with that what you will.

I turned my phone on silent and picked up both it and my wineglass to bring them back to my couch. I couldn't deny that I was happy to have the snow day where, although I still had work that I needed to do, at least I could be by myself to mentally prepare for this dinner.

MY MIND RACED as I glanced at myself one more time before I needed to be out of my apartment to be on time for this "date." The red dress and pumps weren't exactly appropriate for the weather, but with a long coat and hopefully some sort of valet, it would make this evening slightly easier.

The team my mom hired to pull this off had more than done their job, and I barely recognized myself. It was such a difference from the typical look I went with. They'd gone with an eyeshadow that made my blue eyes stand out even more. Although they wanted to, I'd declined the use of fake eyelashes because, while I've worn them to high profile dinners, I didn't want to be paranoid that one would fall off during this dinner. I double-checked the red lipstick I was wearing and made sure that the high, intricate bun they'd thrown my blonde hair into still looked perfect. It did make me look more sophisticated than I'd had outside of some of the dinners I attended with my parents.

I reminded myself repeatedly that I needed to keep my

guard up in order to protect myself from whatever Tristan might say or do. This man was a complete stranger, and I wasn't sure what he was capable of. I grabbed the long black coat that I was planning on wearing, picked up the matching black purse that included everything I needed for the night, and walked out of my apartment.

Thankfully, La Trattoria was only about twenty to twenty-five minutes away from my place, so the drive there wasn't bad. The snow in Brentson had gone from looking pretty on the ground, making it look like a beautiful winter wonderland, to being discolored due to city life. It was to be expected, and I knew we'd have more snow at some point this year to replace the beauty that was lost.

As I stepped out of my car and approached the restaurant, I couldn't help but admire the scene in front of me. The scent of garlic and tomatoes greeted me. I took a deep breath and tried to calm my nerves.

It was easy to see why La Trattoria was the talk of Brentson right now, even looking from the outside. It blended classic and contemporary elements together, including the beautiful stonework that was designed in such a way that made it look modern. The restaurant's name was displayed in a very elegant script that was softly lit from behind the sign.

As I stepped inside the restaurant, I noticed how perfectly the interior blended rustic charm with a modern elegance. The exposed brick contained art that was stunning, and I couldn't help but wonder who'd designed the pieces.

I walked up to the podium and told the hostess I was a part of Tristan Whitmore's party. She gave me a wide smile and walked me toward a table that was in a secluded part of the restaurant. I wondered if that was done by chance or by design.

I wasn't surprised to find that Tristan was already there.

This was it. The moment of truth.

Without a doubt in my mind, I knew this evening was bound to get very interesting.

12

BIANCA

"Hey," Tristan said as he stood up to greet the hostess and me. "You look beautiful."

"Thank you," I replied, feeling a bit flustered. I hoped my face didn't turn the same color as my dress. My nervousness increased tenfold as a result of his compliment.

It was awkward because I, in no way, had any romantic feelings toward him, but I also couldn't voice that at this time. Tristan moved around as I took my seat and helped me push myself closer to the table. It was obvious that he was rolling out all the stops, making me feel even more weird.

"Your waiter will be here momentarily, and if you need anything, please don't hesitate to let us know."

I nodded and eyed the menu until the hostess left. As we each looked through our menus, I could feel the weight of this situation hanging over us like a dark cloud. I tried to distract myself by focusing on the menu hard, but my mind kept thinking about the conversation we were about to have.

"This has to be one of the strangest things you've ever done, huh?"

Tristan's words took me by surprise and forced me to look up at him. I tilted my head to the side as if I was trying to understand what he was saying. He'd temporarily left me speechless, but when my brain caught up, I blurted out the first thing I could think of.

"I didn't imagine being involved in a fake engagement or marriage at my age, so yes, this is one of the strangest things I've ever done."

"All because of these silly photos, right? You know if those photos do surface, I can keep them from getting out. I have a stake in the media game and can make sure they never see the light of day. My connections within the industry would ensure that no one would want to touch them for fear of repercussions. No one wants to get on my bad side."

I stared at him for a moment, shocked and unsure of how to proceed. "B-but in return, you want us to go the whole nine yards with this engagement and marriage."

Tristan shrugged but added nothing more. His ambivalence washed away any sense of relief that I had. I needed to know his ulterior motives.

Before I could ask him, our waiter came to our table, a bright smile on his face. "Good evening, can I take your order?" he asked.

"Yes, that would be great," I said, quickly looking over the menu one more time. "I'll have the Spaghetti alla Carbonara, please. And just a water for me."

"Fantastic. And for you, sir?"

"I'll have the Bistecca alla Fiorentina, medium rare, and a glass of your finest red wine," he ordered, handing his menu back to the waiter.

"Great. I'll get those in for you." The waiter grabbed our

menus, his eyes moving between Tristan and me as if he sensed the tension hanging in the air. He quickly left and we were alone once again.

I tucked a loose piece of hair behind my ear and asked, "Back to what we were talking about earlier?"

Tristan nodded and said, "Sure. After all, this was what we were coming here to discuss."

"While I thank you for offering to make all of this go away, I don't understand why. What do you get out of this except a marriage to someone who isn't halfway through college yet?"

"Don't sell yourself short, Bianca. I have my reasons. I think our partnership will be a very lucrative one." The intensity in his gaze made me want to run out of this restaurant and never look back.

I'd told myself multiple times since my father announced this ruse that there was no way this was happening, and this confirmed it. There was no way things would work out between the two of us, and I refused to be a pawn in whatever game he was playing. Before I could say something else, interrogating him further about his intentions, he cleared his throat and spoke once more.

"Now that we've talked about the heavy things, we should focus on something else. How are things going with school?"

We fell into a somewhat awkward conversation about some friendly topics, but I found myself wishing that I could leave. Thankfully, I was eventually saved when our waiter arrived with our dishes. While we ate our meal, I found myself relaxing slightly, trying to shove down the red flags that had been thrown up during the conversation we'd had earlier in the night. My guard was still up around him, but I felt myself laughing more than I thought I would. Tristan was charming and funny, but I was still convinced that it was all an attempt to disarm my defenses, and I refused to let him complete the job.

An idea popped into my head while we'd taken a break from talking to eat, and I couldn't shove it to the back of my mind and let it fester there without asking it out loud. I finished chewing a bit of my food and placed my fork down. "I don't think I can move on from the reason why we're here tonight. I still want to discuss more in depth about what this whole arrangement would look like."

I tried to mask any contempt I had for all of this in order to not give my real feelings away.

"What else did you want to talk about?" I didn't know Tristan well at all, but he didn't seem annoyed by my desire to go back to the main topic at hand.

"What else is my father getting out of this?"

"What do you mean what else is he getting out of this?"

I tapped my fingers on the table, stalling a moment as I tried to gain a bit of confidence before I blurted out what I'd been thinking.

"The photos are bad, but nothing that wouldn't eventually pass. Politicians come back from worse things all the time, and it had nothing to do with him. So, he must be getting something else out of this that has nothing to do with keeping his daughter safe."

"I shouldn't be surprised you picked up on that. Your father would be taken care of financially, amongst other things, for this arrangement."

"I knew it." It took everything within me not to drop a cuss word or two at the revelation. His reasoning for this engagement and marriage had nothing to do with my behavior, but everything to do with him gaining more money and, I would assume, more power, because he'd have a strong connection with someone who could squash any story about him if anything happened. Including when he launched his bid for higher office after he was done being Mayor of Brentson.

I would swear on everything that my father was the world's biggest asshole, and so was my mother for agreeing to the stunts he liked to pull. While this wasn't the first stunt he'd pulled, this was by far the worst.

"All of this is a big decision and you do have time to make it."

I blinked at him once and stared. If this had been my father sitting in front of me, this conversation would have gone around in circles until I agreed. "I didn't know I had a choice."

"I don't want to drag you kicking and screaming down the aisle. If you decide that this isn't going to work for you, that's fine. Your parents will be another story, but there will be no hard feelings on my end."

This dinner was full of surprises that I couldn't have predicted. At least one thing I couldn't call it was boring. "Thanks, I'll think about it."

I was still firmly against getting married to Tristan, but I now had the potential to buy myself time with all of this, which made me not saying outright I had no intention of being in this union.

We finished our meal in silence, the soft music and the clatter of plates and cutlery the only sounds in the restaurant.

It wasn't an awkward silence, but I was very much lost in my own thoughts, and Tristan allowed me to be.

As we got up to leave, Tristan helped me into my coat, and together we walked to the front of the restaurant, where we waited for the valet to bring my car around. When it pulled up to a stop in front of us, I turned to Tristan.

"Goodnight," I said, my voice barely above a whisper.

"Night, Bianca."

I got into my car and pulled away from the restaurant, feeling slightly more confident than when I entered. Knowing that I actually had a choice changed my thoughts on the situation and gave me even more to think about with regard to moving forward. Now, while I couldn't predict the future, I did feel slightly more optimistic about it.

13

EASTON

A chilled air swept over my skin as I walked into the tiny room. It took everything within me not to clench my jaw because of the cold. My stubbornness refused to let on how much I hated it. Then again, it was unsurprising given where I was. The concrete walls did their job of making the space look physically cold. The room was mostly empty outside of a table and a couple of chairs. If I hadn't known better, I would have assumed I was at a police station. Goose bumps appeared on my arms as I sat down across from the polygraph examiner that was an alum of the Chevaliers.

I'd arrived at the Chevalier Manor for my second initiation task, and I was somewhat regretting it given what I'd walked into. The Chevaliers claimed to value honesty and good character above all else. In order to join, I had to prove my loyalty and my ambition, so I understood the point of this, but that didn't mean I wanted to do it.

The examiner looked me in the eye, and it almost felt as if he could see into my soul. "Are you ready, Mr. Beaumont?"

I stared at the lie detector machine sitting only a few inches away from me. The nerves that I'd kept under wraps since I'd arrived here burst to the surface, ready to erupt at any moment. "Yes," I said. I did everything I could not to show any fear over what was about to happen.

He attached the sensors to my fingers. "Remember, honesty is the most important thing here. Lying will have consequences."

If I wasn't aware of the seriousness of this task, I would have waved him off. Consequences. I knew all about that.

The examiner leaned forward in his chair with not a speck of a smile on his face. "First question. Is your name Easton Beaumont?"

"Yes," I answered confidently as he gave me a softball question.

"Do you attend Brentson University?"

I nodded slightly. "Yes."

"Have you told anyone about the Chevaliers or this initiation process?"

"No," I said firmly, quickly noticing that we were getting into the serious questions now. My heart thumped hard as the sensors registered my response. I was pretty sure it had skipped a beat. I thought back to what I told Bianca, but she'd already known I was going through this.

He made a note on his clipboard. "Do you have any secret allegiances that could conflict with the Chevaliers?"

"No." I took a deep breath, trying to stay calm. But my thoughts swirled with doubts when normally they wouldn't have. This whole session was fucking with me, and I was sure that was done by design.

The examiner studied me, to the point where I was

wondering if he was peering into my mind. "You seem nervous, Mr. Beaumont. Is there something you wish to confess before we continue?"

I hesitated. "I'm no more nervous than anyone else who is hooked up to a machine with you staring them down."

The man in front of me chuckled. "Very well."

He wrote something else down in his book. I wished I could move my body so that I could read what he was writing. What did he suspect?

The examiner leaned back, but his gaze only grew in intensity. "Have you ever betrayed someone's trust?"

I swallowed hard as a memory assaulted me. The look on Bianca's face when I admitted to the deal.

I tried to force the memories away, but with the examiner watching me closely, I knew there was no use. He'd figure it out anyway.

"Yes," I whispered. "I have."

"Tell me about it," he said as if it was the easiest thing in the world.

I licked my lips, but I knew I had no choice. The sensors would reveal the truth anyway.

"I kept something from someone I cared about, and it hurt her immensely. I regret doing that now. I wish I could take it back."

"Let's move on to our next question. Would you choose loyalty to the society over your personal relationships?"

I thought about it for a moment and wondered if this was the cause of the hesitation Bianca was getting from Nash when she asked him to find out about the Chevaliers connection to Iris's disappearance. Apparently, she was right to think Nash might hide some stuff from her.

"I will." I tried my best to keep my pulse steady as the doubts started to creep in.

He wrote something else down.

This process continued and my nervousness began to lessen with each subsequent question. As long as none of the questions made me think of Bianca, I had no problem with answering. Finally, I heard the words I'd been waiting for.

"The test is over. You may go now."

His expression gave nothing away as I stared at him while I processed the words he'd said. He walked over to me and began removing the wires and the other apparatuses that he'd put on my body.

That was it? Everything was done? I'd completed the task, and I had no idea how I'd done.

"How do I know if I passed?"

The examiner sat down and removed his glasses and said, "You'll receive a notification of some sort."

I took that as my dismissal and stood up and left the cold room. No one stopped me as I left Chevalier Manor, but I did see Nash for a brief moment. He gave me a small nod, his face showing indifference as I walked to the door. I didn't break our eye contact until I closed the door behind me. I couldn't help but think that the last time I'd been here, I was being dragged in with a hood over my head because he wanted to beat me up for messing with Bianca.

But with the fresh air flowing over my face and reaching my lungs, I was able to exhale slowly, giving me the ability to release the tension that had settled all over my body. The interrogation was over, and now I just needed to wait for the results.

The more I'd gotten involved in the Chevaliers, the more I

realized that this was a brotherhood bound by secrets and power, and they would use any means necessary to get what they wanted. The end for them was a bottomless pit, and they would go to the ends of the earth in order to meet their objectives. I both admired that and was concerned about what it would mean for me if everything came crashing down.

Sometime later, I stumbled into my apartment, mentally tired from all the questions I'd been forced to answer. I made a beeline for my couch, determined to veg out in front of the television until I needed to go to bed.

Almost as soon as I turned on my television, a commercial featuring Diana Caldwell and Van Henson caught my eye. Bianca's father looked tired and worn, his suit rumpled and his hair unkempt, and I'm sure that was done by design. Diana, on the other hand, appeared to have all the confidence and power one could muster, her tailored suit highlighting that she was more than ready to be mayor of Brentson. There was a quick change of scenery that featured children playing at a playground in the background while Diana walked down a street in Brentson.

"Van Henson has failed Brentson," Diana declared, cutting through the silence in my place. Her eyes flashed with anger as she looked into the camera. She gestured dramatically with a sweep of her arm to showcase the scene behind her— children laughing, parents talking, Brentson's community as a whole. "Our town and our children deserve better than his empty promises and the salacious secrets that he keeps."

She made sure to pause for dramatic effect, letting her words sink in for the viewer.

I sat up from the slouching position I'd been in while lying on my couch as an idea formed in my head. Could

Diana be behind the leaked photos? Was she using under-handed ways to try and undermine Van Henson's campaign?

It would make the most sense. She was his opponent, and she had a lot to gain.

"We deserve a leader who is transparent, has no problem being held accountable, and one who truly cares about all of the residents of Brentson," Diana continued, her tone shifting from angry to compassionate.

I turned off the commercial before I could hear anything else. I needed to focus on any evidence that pointed to her being the suspect, not getting caught up in maybe this or potentially that.

I grabbed my laptop and booted it up. I started digging through news articles and social media posts, not sure what I was looking for or what I was hoping to find. However, my thoughts kept drifting back to the commercial. Diana's words lingered in my mind, and I wasn't sure why.

Could she have hired someone to hack my computer or to follow Bianca around and take those photos? I wasn't sure how many photos were sent to Van or which ones they were, which could be helpful in telling us one way or another.

How could I figure out a way to see the photos? Did it make sense for me to go and talk to Diana?

More importantly, I needed to decide if and when I was going to bring Bianca into this.

14

BIANCA

I needed to go to my parents this weekend to debrief them on my dinner date with Tristan. As I parked my car and walked toward their home, I could feel the tightness in my chest growing stronger. My childhood home, which should have been a beacon of safety, almost reminded me of a prison now.

Unsurprisingly, nothing had changed since I was home last. What also hadn't changed was the feeling of dread that I had every time I stepped foot in here.

Part of me still wanted to try to fight against this engagement with all my heart. How could I make them understand that this marriage was not what was best for me or our family? I knew there was no chance in hell of me getting through to my father because of the money aspect and who knew what else. But maybe, just maybe, I could hold out hope for my mother. In regard to this, she might be the easiest to flip and then I might be able to have some leverage here.

My thoughts were interrupted by the sound of footsteps,

which were soon followed by my mother entering the hall-way. As always, my mother looked put together, her hair perfectly coiffed and her clothing crisp and clean. She looked like the epitome of a perfect politician's wife. Although nothing on the surface showed this, beneath it all, I knew there was a fierce determination to maintain our family's reputation and lifestyle at all costs.

She was carrying what looked to be a tray that had tea and cookies on it. How ironic that she would serve something like this when I wasn't the biggest fan of tea. My eyes focused on her smile, which looked anything but natural and her stare which showed a hint of sadness.

I followed her into the living room and watched as she set the tray down on the coffee table.

"Thanks for coming home," she said. "Please, take a seat."

Deep down, I could feel this wasn't going to go well, but if I didn't try again before I took action on my own, I would regret it.

"So, how was your dinner date with Tristan?"

"It was fine, but I still have no intention of marrying him."

"Now, Bianca—"

"No. I know you and Dad want this arrangement, but this is my life. I don't want to do this, so I won't."

My mother's face crumbled, and I felt the guilt settle in my stomach. I couldn't help but wonder if she was about to turn on the waterworks. "You have to realize this marriage is the best thing for our family's future."

My frustration was quickly growing. How could she not see how wrong she was? How wrong this was? *Why doesn't she see what she is doing to me?*

"Mom, I thought you would be on my side," I said, feeling

foolish for holding out hope for such a thing. I'd always held onto hope that one day she'd choose me, but apparently that wasn't today.

When my father entered the room, I could almost feel a shift in the temperature as his stern eyes fixated on me. "Bianca, we've discussed this already. The marriage will happen, whether you like it or not."

I stood up, my fists clenched to my sides, but ready to swing if necessary. "I said no. You're not going to control my life and force me into a situation that I don't want to be in."

"I've already told her this marriage will secure her future and help us maintain our standing within the community," my mom chimed in.

I turned to her and said, "But what about what I want? What about what makes me happy?"

"Sometimes we have to make sacrifices in life. Maybe you'll grow to love Tristan."

I had to be living in an alternate universe. Why did I even bother coming here?

"Hold on." My father put his hand up as a sign for my mother to stop talking. It was beyond rude, but my father didn't have his politician mask on so this is what we got. "What is it that you want, Bianca?"

"I don't know. I want to care about the person I marry. Hell, I want love," I said, hoping that I didn't start crying. "I want love, Dad. I don't want to be stuck in a loveless marriage just because it'll save your asses. I don't care if those photos are released because there's nothing in those pictures that I'm doing that hasn't been done by countless other college students before."

"Watch your mouth," my father said as he frowned and

glared at me. His stance made me wonder if he was going to strike me, but he seemed to keep his composure. "And love? You're being naïve. Love doesn't put food on the table. Love doesn't win elections. Love doesn't build a legacy. You need to think about the bigger picture here."

I swallowed my tears and steadied myself by taking deep breaths in through my nose and out through my mouth. I needed to remain calm. "What I need to be thinking about is the fact that this isn't about the photos at all. This is so you can make even more money and who knows what else."

"You don't know what the hell you're talking about," my father replied.

By the deepening color in his cheeks, I knew that I was right.

"You can try to lie to me, and potentially Mom, because who knows how much you actually tell her, but we all know the truth. Regardless, I'm an adult, this is my life, and I decide what happens in it. If you're so gung-ho about all of this, why don't you divorce Mom and then you can marry Tristan. No one's stopping you from doing that."

My father scoffed, his face darkening considerably. He took several steps toward me and this time, I was convinced that he was going to hit me based on the speed that he was traveling. I'd pushed him so close to the edge, that out of the corner of my eye, I saw my mother get up as if she might interfere if need be. I couldn't help but wonder if she was getting up to protect me or to protect my father from himself.

Instead, my father stared at me with an intensity that made my blood rush to my ears. "I hate that I have to say this again, but I'll tell you one more time. You will do as I say and marry Tristan or else I will ruin your life without remorse.

You may think that you know what you're doing and what it takes to succeed in this world, but trust me when I say that you don't. Your mistakes have the potential to ruin the lives of those closest to you. So cut this nonsense out and fall in line."

When my mother didn't say a peep to agree or contradict what my father said, I hated that I was hurt, but also found it interesting that she didn't jump to his defense. However, I didn't have any time to explore that now.

"Whatever," I said, as I looked toward the exit. "Do what you want. But know that I won't go down without a fight. You can bet everything you own that I'll find a way out of this, even if it means going against you and everything you stand for."

I side-stepped my father so that I could leave and stormed out of my childhood home without taking a moment to look at the two people who had raised me. Fuck that and fuck them. I could hear my mother's voice calling after me as I walked away, but I didn't turn back. There was nothing left to discuss. I was going to do whatever it took to maintain control over my own life, even if it meant going against everything my family stood for.

I jumped into my car without another word and closed the doors behind me. I took out my phone and sent a text message to the one person I knew could distract me from the pain I was feeling.

Me: Are you home?

Easton: Yes, why?

Me: Because I'll be over there shortly.

15

BIANCA

I ran a hand across my cheek as I wiped the tear that fell from the corner of my eye. I put both hands back on the steering wheel and clenched the wheel between my fingers as rage simmered within me.

It had taken me a long time to get to this point, but this was what it felt like to be completely helpless when it came to changing someone's opinion of you. How could they be so cruel? Especially to their own flesh and blood. How could I be so stupid as to think that I could go back there and change their minds after I showed good faith by going out to dinner with Tristan? They'd confirmed once more that I was nothing more than a pawn in their sick little game of politics and power.

But that was now behind me, at least for now.

I was on my way to Easton's to think about anything but my parents.

Easton.

My chest tightened at the thought of him, making it

slightly hard to breathe. A confusing mix of emotions swirled through me as I pictured him.

Anger.

Happiness.

Betrayal.

Salvation.

Melded within everything was a hunger I couldn't satisfy. An ache for the one thing that made me feel alive.

Him.

His lips. His touch. The way he could make me forget about every issue and every problem. Nothing mattered but us and the pleasure we found in each other's arms.

Should I be doing this? Probably not. I knew it would only make things worse in the long run. But right then, I suspected it was a better option than drinking until I passed out.

I shouldn't go to him. I knew that. Potentially trading one addiction for another probably wasn't the smartest plan, but I'd deal with that another time.

I was headed to the one person who could set me free tonight.

As I drove through the dark streets of Brentson, I couldn't focus on any one thought outside of how quickly I could make it to Easton's.

Each mile that I drove closer to his apartment, the fluttering in my stomach became more pronounced, as though a kaleidoscope of butterflies had taken up residence there. I was about to step into another world, one ruled by the pleasure that Easton sparked within me. Every fiber of my being was aware of the promise and the danger that lay behind his door.

I let out a deep sigh and flicked on my turn signal to let the cars behind me know I was turning into this parking lot. As I pulled up to the front of his apartment building, my stomach lodged in my throat. For a moment, I sat staring through the thick glass doors leading to the lobby before I gathered enough courage to step out of my vehicle.

I walked toward the lobby and saw Easton come into view. He'd been waiting for me in the lobby because I hadn't told him how far away I was from his place. That caused my heart to beat a little faster than it had the entire drive over here.

When my eyes met his, my breath caught in my throat. I knew I had made the right decision. Tonight, the rest of the world could burn for all I cared. I was allowed to be selfish and not care about what anyone else thought for just one night.

Without a word, Easton strolled over to me, took my hand, then turned around and led me back to the elevator bank. We waited for our ride in silence, and the tension between the two of us went from zero to a million in less than ten seconds. I was glad we hadn't said a word to each other because I wouldn't be liable for my actions.

We remained quiet the entire ride up the elevator, and it wasn't until I heard his front door click shut behind us that it was as if a light switch went off.

For a long moment we just looked at each other, the air between us sparking due to the tension that was about to overflow.

"Bianca," he said, and it came across as a low growl.

The way he said my name as his eyes once again met mine was like a rough caress. Danger blared from every corner of my brain, but I didn't care. The heat I noticed in his eyes told me I wasn't the only one who was feeling this way.

I couldn't wait any longer.

I dropped my bag and launched myself at him. He had no problem lifting me up so that my lips could easily reach his. I wrapped my legs around his waist, pulling him closer to me as he stole my breath away. I melted against him, enjoying the feel of his touch on me. His hands made their way into my hair, lightly pulling on my ponytail as his lips punished mine. The next thing I knew, my hair was falling on my shoulders.

I let out a soft groan when my ass touched his kitchen counter, and when Easton gave me one of his own, the sound vibrated through my soul.

Why did it feel as if it had been years since we last kissed? It was as if my body was needy for his and I was finally giving into my craving.

Sure, there were plenty of things we needed to discuss, but I was over talking right now. Action was the only language I wanted to speak as we both gave into our desires.

He pulled off my jacket without stopping our kiss. I put my hands on his cheeks to anchor him to me, but he snatched his head away. I only had a moment to process what was happening before I felt his hand grab the collar of my button-down shirt and pull, forcing the buttons of my blouse to fly in every direction, exposing my black lace bra.

My nipples hardened under his gaze, and I bit the corner of my lip.

"Did you wear this because you were coming to see me today?"

"No. Not everything is about you, asshole."

"But your pussy is all about me, isn't it?"

Easton had me there. His lips slammed into mine again, showing me exactly who was in charge tonight, but that didn't mean I was immediately giving in. He stepped between my legs as our tongues danced together, competing for who was going to have control. My hands roamed over his chest before he pulled away once more to remove his shirt and toss it to who knows where.

He went back to kissing me. This time, my eyes widened as he sucked on the sensitive skin of my neck. For a split second, I wondered if he was going to give me a hickey in an attempt to lay claim to me. While I normally would have been irritated, and it wouldn't look good for someone who might end up being engaged to someone else, I didn't care.

"You don't know how badly I want to shove my cock into your mouth and watch you attempt to take all of me."

"Then do it," I said. We were spending too much time talking for my liking.

"Get on your knees, princess."

Easton moved away to give me space, and as I sank down to my knees in front of him, he undid his belt and jeans.

His cock sprang free, and I was left staring at it for a moment before I licked the head of his dick. I heard Easton suck in a deep breath before his hands ended up in my hair, pulling it back into a makeshift ponytail. Knowing that he had the ability to see everything spurred me on as I took his cock into my mouth.

I made sure to take him deeper, inch by inch, determined to show him that I could take anything that he could throw at me. Our relationship, or whatever you wanted to call it, might be on a timer, but I was determined to make the best of this enemies-with-benefits situation.

Was he still my enemy? If he leaked those photos to my father, he sure as hell was.

I gagged briefly on his cock, bringing me back to the task at hand before I took more of him, praying that my gag reflex would keep its cool.

When his hips started to move, his cock moved with them and the groan that fell from his lips was music to my ears. I quickly caught on that he was beginning to fuck my face, and I did my best to relax, preparing myself for what would eventually come.

And I meant *come* quite literally.

"Fuck, princess. How did I fucking know you'd be so good at this?"

I couldn't answer him because my mouth was preoccupied. He didn't pick up speed yet even though I wanted to tell him he could. If he was enjoying the way this was going right now, who was I to ruin our fun?

My brain kept jumping between the scene that was playing out through my own eyes and wondering if he planned on coming in my mouth or in my pussy. My attention was drawn back to him when he ran a hand down my cheek, and I looked up at him with wide eyes.

I could tell that he was barely hanging on, and I reveled in that. This whole scene that was happening? It was all because of me.

I couldn't deny that I was proud of it.

His speed picked up and I heard him grunt. For whatever reason, it seemed as if he was trying to hold it together, when all I wanted to do was watch him lose control because of me.

"You're going to swallow every single last drop," he said through gritted teeth.

In this moment, I was willing to do whatever he said as long as it ended with him fucking me. I moaned with his cock still in my mouth, and he hissed in response. He tightened his grip on my hair before he let out a low moan as he fell apart.

When he was done, I kneeled there awkwardly on the floor while I watched him try to collect himself. I wasn't sure what to do outside of standing up and trying to fix my shirt. Then again, there was no use in doing that because who knew where all the buttons landed.

"Did you think that was it, baby?"

I froze in place. "I—I—"

"Go down the hall to my bedroom. I'm nowhere near done with you yet."

16

BIANCA

Easton and I engaged in a small stare down before an idea appeared into my mind. Since I had his full and undivided attention, I decided to make the most of it.

Without breaking eye contact, I teasingly shrugged off my blouse, revealing all of my black lace bra underneath. Easton's eyes darkened as he watched me intently.

I moved toward him, and Easton couldn't help but take a step forward to meet me halfway. When we were standing face-to-face once more, his gaze traveled from my face down to my bra-clad chest numerous times before finally settling on my lips.

Without warning, he leaned forward and captured my lips in an electrifying kiss that left me breathless yet wanting for more.

I put some distance between us by pushing on his chest and said, "I guess I'll head to the bedroom now."

I turned on my heel and strolled down the hall until I reached the bedroom. My eyes drifted around the room as I took in what was his private sanctuary. What I hadn't expected was to feel two strong arms wrap around my waist and lift me up.

I squealed in surprise, briefly feeling like I was a little girl again as he tossed me down on the bed.

My body sank into the comforter, and I sighed as I felt its softness against my skin. I couldn't help but stare as he leaned over me. At first, I felt him graze my neck with his nose, followed by his lips, sending shivers down my spine. He paused at my mouth, making sure to show me that he owned my lips. The featherlight kisses continued down my body, pausing when he reached my lacy bra. I had to give my past self a pat on the back for choosing to wear this today.

Once he reached my breasts, it was as if something spurred him into action. The haphazard way that we were going at each other when I first walked through the door returned. I didn't know what had caused the change, but I was more than happy to embrace it because I wanted him inside of me right now.

He left a kiss on the top of each breast before yanking my bra down, exposing my breasts to him. I heard him mumble something under his breath before he teased both nipples using his thumbs and index fingers to the point where they were as hard as pebbles, sending jolts of electricity to my pussy.

"Why are you so fucking beautiful?"

I heard the words loud and clear this time and watched as he stared at me in amazement. I didn't have an answer to his question, and he stared at me as if he couldn't believe I was here. Hell, in a similar fashion, I couldn't believe I was lying underneath him either.

It was funny how life worked out.

He slapped my breast lightly, causing it to jiggle, then he wasted no time bending down to suck my nipple into his mouth.

My fingers ended up tangled in his hair as I arched my back, in hopes of anchoring his mouth to my chest. He did more than satisfy my craving for his touch, and I gasped out when he lightly bit my nipple before licking it to soothe the pain. The mixture of what felt like hot and cold was enough to set my whole body ablaze.

He drew his focus to my other nipple so as not to leave it without attention.

He then trailed his kisses down my body, leaving my skin burning in his wake.

The anticipation of what was to come was killing me. I wanted him so badly it hurt.

He paused once he reached my pants. As I felt him unbutton them, I was confused when he didn't remove them completely. I moved my head so that I could look down at him with a raised eyebrow. I wanted to know what he had planned next.

He responded by giving me a smirk that said more than any words could before he sank down lower. He rubbed small circles on my inner thighs, teasing me in preparation for what was to come.

I couldn't help but groan out when he worked his way up before stopping at the top of my pants. His fingers gripped onto the sides of my pants and snatched them off, showing that any patience he might have had was no longer in the building.

"I want you on your knees. Flip over."

His commands sent a thrill up and down my spine. I didn't waste another second and turned over so that I was on all fours before him.

One of his fingers ran down my back before reaching my ass. He spanked me twice, once on each cheek. My breathing became more ragged as his hand continued its journey.

"What's this?" Easton asked as he ran his fingers across my slit, teasing me through my panties. "You're soaking through your panties, princess."

"What are you going to do about it?"

"Fuck you until you realize who owns this cunt," he said as he slid them down, removing the last barrier between him and my needy pussy.

My mouth dropped open as he got off the bed.

I turned my head to watch him remove the rest of his clothes. I was caught in a trance as his dick sprung out, and when he started fisting himself, I nearly lost my mind.

I was brought back to the night he'd taken my virginity and how much this moment differed from that night. Then I'd been a nervous wreck, and now I felt more confident than ever.

It was as if everything that I was dealing with ceased to exist temporarily and the only thing that mattered was the small bubble that Easton and I were creating inside his apartment.

I automatically assumed that the next thing I would feel was his cock inside of me, but he surprised me by using a finger to play with my pussy instead. I pushed back on him as he wasted no time picking up his speed, driving me closer and closer to the edge.

"Do you want to come right now or on my dick, princess?"

I bit my lip as I tried to think of my answer. Thankfully, one just fell out of my mouth. "On your cock."

"Excellent answer."

He removed his finger, and I waited with bated breath as I heard him grab a condom.

"I'm on birth control."

I watched as Easton froze as if he was considering what I said.

"Does this mean what I think it means?"

"It does," I said as I stuck my hand between my legs to play with my clit while he stared.

I chuckled when I saw him toss the condom over his shoulder, but it quickly turned into a groan when he pushed his cock inside of me. Without the barrier between us, I was shell-shocked at how different it felt, and that we were actually doing this.

His thrusts started immediately and were perfectly timed. My moans went from low to practically screaming the harder he pounded into me. He moved his hips in such a way that it felt as if every inch of his cock was driving into me over and over again. I almost cried from the intensity of the sensations that he was stirring within me.

My hands instinctively clenched the bed sheets because I needed something to hold on to. They'd become the only way I had a grip on reality because I felt like I would drift away due to all the pleasure coursing through my veins.

His motions only intensified as each second passed, the sound of our fucking the only thing that surrounded us. Soon I was on the verge of an explosive orgasm. When it finally took over, I felt like my body had locked up in preparation for what would be our endgame. Easton must have realized what was happening too because he started thrusting harder and faster until we both sailed over the edge together.

I didn't care that when I fell over, he did too, with his weight crushing me as we both tried to catch our breaths.

This feeling was absolutely magical, and I couldn't wait to do it again.

I soon drifted off to sleep, my body completely spent from Easton. I didn't know how long it was before I woke up again and I turned to watch Easton's face as he slept. I couldn't help but smile at how peaceful he looked while sleeping and an idea popped into my head.

I moved my hand until it touched what I was looking for. I scrolled through the apps on my phone until I found my camera.

Taking a deep breath, I snapped a picture of us both snuggled up together in bed. It felt weird taking this picture without his knowledge, but I needed it for security.

And if I played my cards right, it might just get me out of this sham of an engagement.

17

BIANCA

fter a late night, due to both of us being insatiable, I fell into a dreamless sleep that was probably the most peaceful I'd had in quite some time. I didn't stir until a pulsing sensation grew between my legs, but it didn't last long. The light buzzing noise that surrounded me was still low enough that I was willing to turn back over in an attempt to go back to sleep.

At first, I tried to drift off again but then the feeling between my legs became too powerful to ignore. What was it? It almost felt like... like something was running up and down my pussy, the touches light enough for me to recognize something, but not enough for me to care to wake up.

The sensation came again, stronger this time, and I moaned softly. I was almost fully awake now and I could feel my hips moving on their own.

I must still be dreaming. This can't be real.

But it felt real. Too real. My breathing became harsher as the vibration increased. That was when all of my senses went into rapid-fire mode, and I realized where the soft buzzing noise I heard was coming from. I gasped out loud as I fisted the bed sheets, realization dawning down on me. I opened my eyes and was greeted by darkness, but the sensations that were flowing through my body made me not care. I wanted to tear off whatever was across my eyes and to see Easton, but I also didn't want this fantasy to end.

When the vibration increased once again, it was like nothing I'd experienced before, and that included the fun I'd had with my own small toy collection. A scream flew out from my lips as my back arched and I let my body give in to my orgasm. The waves seemed to go on forever, and I never wanted it to end.

As I came down from that high, panting and trembling, it was then that I realized something else. There was the feeling of someone watching me, wanting me.

"Easton?" I said just before I licked my suddenly dry lips.

"Who else would it be?"

"Was that a vibrator?"

"Maybe."

I could hear the grin in his voice. When I moved to take off the blindfold, Easton grabbed my wrist.

"Keep it on."

"Why?" I was slightly puzzled by his desire to keep my eyes covered. I wanted to see him too.

"Because this is how I want you." And he didn't offer up any other explanation.

His fingers traced an imaginary line along the inside of my knee. Even that small touch was erotic as fuck. "I debated with myself whether I should wake you up or not. And while you looked so peaceful sleeping there, I couldn't resist hearing the sounds of your beautiful moans once more."

"I'm not complaining. At all."

"Good. Then shall we continue?"

I chuckled when Easton asked his question with the fakest British accent I'd ever heard. "I don't think I can... again."

"You don't think you can *what* again?"

I took a deep breath before I blurted it out again. "I don't think I can come again."

Easton waited a beat before he replied, "Challenge accepted."

I squealed and said, "This is so wrong." I could feel his hand sliding up my thigh and I had a good idea where his final destination was.

"How wrong does this feel, Bianca?" he asked as he began to rub slow circles over my clit before he suddenly stopped.

I groaned in protest. It wasn't worth me trying to fight this or him anymore.

"You want this as much as I do, and you know it. I can feel your wetness and I absolutely love it."

His fingers began to tease me once more and I tossed my head back involuntarily. I clenched the sheets as he built my body up again; this time it seemed as if I was already halfway to the edge before he started to play with me once more. This was all happening too quickly.

When Easton added his tongue to the party, I grew tense from the pleasure and anticipation. I knew exactly how this would end and I wasn't convinced that I was ready for it, but he more than likely wouldn't take no for an answer. He ran his tongue along my slit, teasing me with an appetizer when I really wanted the full meal.

My hands ended up in his hair in an attempt to hold him in place. He made sure to play with my clit and had no problem making sure that every inch of my pussy had received all the attention that it deserved.

I gasped out loud when he began to fuck me with his fingers, but it was from surprise versus pain. I cried out as he plunged his fingers in and out of me, taking time in between to play with my G-spot. I rode his hand, begging for a release without saying the words. The pressure that was building within me was a ticking time bomb, ready to explode at a moment's notice.

Having the blindfold on seemed to only heighten my other senses, which was to be expected. My will to resist this man shattered and I surrendered to the desire that ruled my heart.

"Come for me again," he demanded.

I followed his command perfectly. I swirled out of control as my climax hit me hard, and it was several moments before I was able to think again, let alone speak.

My body trembled slightly, yet I felt as if I was in a haze, floating just above my body without any signs of coming down. The warmth that spread through me made me smile, happy to have been able to experience all of this.

I gasped when I realized that he wasn't done. He pushed my legs further apart and I could feel the head of his cock teasing my entrance. There was no way that I'd be ready to go again, right?

He took his time sliding into me, I assumed accounting for the fact that my pussy was probably sore from his earlier ministrations as well as the fun we had the night before.

My mouth dropped open as he moved, but not a sound left my lips. Euphoric was the best way I could describe this experience. Coming here was the best thing I could have done after dealing with my parents and their bullshit.

Once he was all the way inside of me, he only stayed still for a moment before he slowly withdrew himself and then slammed back into me. My moans turned into cries every time he pounded into me. Every little adjustment he made only increased the sparks between us. My nerves felt as if they were frayed.

I grabbed Easton's shoulders as the pressure built up within me. When my next orgasm hit me, my mind was blown that it was number three. As the orgasm tore through me, I managed to find and grip Easton's shoulders as tight as I could. Without a doubt, I was leaving a mark.

Once again, it felt as if I was having an out-of-body experience as Easton continued fucking me. When his rhythm grew erratic, I knew he was closing in on his own release.

A low groan fell from his lips as he thrust into me one final time, and I shivered in response. Feeling him explode inside of me was so erotic that all I could do was replay the moment in my mind over and over again.

For a moment, neither one of us moved as we both tried to catch our breaths. I moved my hands from his shoulders to his hair, giving him a light scalp massage.

"I think I've died," Easton said with a sigh. "And it's all because of you."

"But wasn't it a lovely way to go?"

Easton let out a breathless laugh before he kissed me on

the lips. This kiss was slow and sensual as he slowly pulled the blindfold from my eyes. I blinked several times as I got used to the light and was struck by the look he was giving me. The tenderness that I saw reflected in his eyes made me panic slightly.

"I'm going to do everything in my power to prove to you that I didn't leak those photos of you. I swear."

The sincerity in his eyes and words made me feel slightly emotional. It made me want to believe that he was telling me the truth even though a smidge of doubt lingered.

Easton shifted his body so that he could get up, and I immediately felt the loss of him. However, even I had to admit that I needed a break after the marathon of sex we'd had.

It took a few minutes to clean up because Easton said that I shouldn't lift a finger and that he would take care of it all. Once we were settled, Easton pulled me into his side so that I could lay on his chest, reminding me again of the night he took my virginity. His fingers traced imaginary figures on my skin, and I enjoyed the sound of his heart beating under my ear.

Though the outside world felt as if it was burning down, here I felt happy and whole. Sure, the Tristan thing was lingering in the background, but I hadn't said yes to our arrangement so nothing I did over the last two days was wrong.

Or so I was telling myself.

I moved slightly to get a better look at Easton because there were still some things we needed to discuss.

"Have you heard anything about Iris?"

Easton shook his head, and my heart sank. I'd been hoping for something more by now.

"I should have another meeting at the Chevalier Manor later this week because we'll find out if we made the cut shortly."

That's right. We were coming up to the end of the semester. "Just as long as you tell me about anything you find as soon as you can."

"I promise you I will. Speaking of things I need to tell you, could it be possible that Diana Caldwell is the one who leaked the photos of you?"

I was taken aback by the question. "I mean it's possible, but she would have to have spies on me and—"

My words died on my lips as I sat up. I jumped out of the bed before Easton could grab me.

"Where are you going?"

He was forced to yell it because I'd already sprinted out of his bedroom, naked I might add. But my lack of clothing wasn't about to get in the way of me getting the item I needed.

I didn't respond to him because I was too busy looking for something. When I realized that I'd already brought it into the bedroom last night, I walked back into that room and grabbed the device with a slight blush on my face.

I scrolled through my text messages on my phone until I found the ones I wanted to show Easton. They were all from the person with the unknown number, including a brand new text.

Unknown Number: Might want to check on that brake light. Wouldn't want to get pulled over outside of E's apartment.

"So these text messages prove that I've been getting stalked. Now you're making me wonder if it's possible that Diana is doing this or hired someone to do so."

Easton read through the messages several times before he turned to look me right in the eyes. "Whoever is sending you these is going to have to answer to me."

18

EASTON

I opened the front door of my parents' home and took a deep breath. I was greeted by the smell of roasted duck. It seemed as if tonight's dinner was going to be a special occasion and I was pretty happy to have a home cooked meal courtesy of our cook.

"Hey, Dad," I said as I took a seat in the dining room opposite my father. He looked up from his phone and gave me a small smile.

"Hey, good of you to join us," he said, slowly leaning back in his chair. "What's new with you?"

I swallowed a piece of duck, enjoying the taste for a moment before I spoke. "I'm in the process of trying out to become a Chevalier."

My father's mouth dropped open slightly, showcasing the fact that I'd actually surprised him. It was rare that it happened, so I was somewhat proud of the achievement.

"I'm proud of you." My father lifted his glass, the crimson wine sloshing inside. "I'm shocked you joined, given that

Nash was already a shoo-in for the top position for next year, or so Van was bragging about at a party a few weeks ago."

I tried to keep my voice even as I replied with a light chuckle. "I'm not competing with Nash in that regard anymore, Dad."

He didn't need to know that we'd literally gotten into a fistfight recently.

My father nodded slowly, but I could see a slight look of confusion on his face. "You know that's not how things work here. He probably sees you as his competition anyway. After all, he was raised by Van Henson."

I wasn't sure how much he was raised by Van if I was being honest. With how much focus has been put on his political career by both he and his wife, I didn't know how much time had been left for their children.

Before I could respond, I watched as my mother walked into the room and took a seat next to my father. My father cleared his throat and said, "Amelia, Easton is in the process of becoming a Chevalier."

Mom looked at me somewhat skeptically before turning to look at my father. "I don't know much about them, but from what we heard, are we sure this is a good idea?"

Dad put his hand over Mom's and gave it a squeeze. "I know it's not the safest organization to be a part of, but we also have to trust his judgment."

I didn't blame her for being concerned.

My father sipped his wine, and as he was putting it back down, he asked, "Do you think you have what it takes to be a Chevalier? I know you can't share with us what is going on, but how is it going?"

"Absolutely. So far things have been challenging, but

nothing too bad," I said as I thought about the fact that I had to beat up some drones and pass a lie detector test. "We'll see what the final challenge brings."

My father smiled. "If you want or need any help with this, Van is probably willing to help. He now owes me a favor anyway, and I assume you can't ask Nash to help you because he would probably be one of the people deciding if you get to join or not."

I sat there, slightly stunned by my father's suggestion. I had never even considered asking Van for help because I didn't think I needed it, but it might not be a bad idea. His connection to the Chevaliers could help me find out more information about Iris for Bianca.

Still, I was hesitant about taking him up on his offer. From what I'd heard over the years, Van was not the most trustworthy person in town. Although he owed my father a favor, I wasn't sure if that would be enough to override any ulterior motives he might have.

I put my fork down and said, "Why does he owe you a favor?"

"We did end up donating to his reelection campaign. A large sum."

My mother must have noticed my expression because she said softly, "If you don't want to reach out to him, then you don't have to do it."

I appreciated Mom's kind and understanding words. While shoving another bite of food into my mouth, I let my father's offer sit out there without me confirming or denying what I wanted to do.

We ate in silence for a bit before I looked up and watched my father play with the wedding ring he'd placed on my mother's left hand decades ago. Their love felt too pure for this conversation we were having about the Chevaliers. I wasn't sure how much information they had about the organization and the darkness that lurked beneath the surface of the society that collected wealthy men like a baseball card collector. If they really knew, I highly doubted they would want me joining the organization.

"I think I would like to have a meeting with Van," I said smoothly. "The Chevaliers will open more doors, opportunities, and connections for me, and I don't want to mess it up." What I was saying was a half-truth, but my parents smiled, happy with my response.

"Speaking of Henson's campaign, did you see the new commercial from Diana Caldwell?"

My father dabbed at the corner of his mouth with a napkin. "I did. She hit Van pretty hard, and it will be interesting to see how effective it is. I admire her tenacity if I'm being honest."

I nodded, agreeing with his assessment. Diana was intelligent and charismatic, so I wasn't surprised that she'd decided on the approach she had.

"Have you spoken to Van about the commercial?"

My father shook his head. "We haven't seen the Hensons since the commercial first aired."

"I'm getting lunch with Elizabeth tomorrow. While we don't normally talk politics, I'd be shocked if this doesn't come up," Mom added.

"It might be worth trying to get on Van's calendar as soon as possible because I'm sure he's going to get distracted with a response to Diana's claims," said my father.

Dad had a good point. It would be potentially hard to get

a meeting with Van. I doubted he had much free time, and the fact that he was in the middle of a political campaign didn't help. But Dad could reach out and try to schedule a meeting with him. Then again, depending on how much my parents donated to the campaign, he might be willing to talk immediately.

I nodded, understanding what he was saying, but I still wanted to take a moment to think about it. "If he asked you, what advice would you give him?"

My father thought for a moment before speaking, "Now, while I'm not a politician, I believe the best way to handle this situation is to respond to her allegations and be open and honest with his constituents. Attacking Diana isn't the answer because, in the end, it's about the citizens of Brentson. If people know that Van is willing to listen and take their opinions into consideration and correct the record, then they are more likely to trust him and believe in his message. Thankfully nothing she said was all that bad."

My mind immediately jumped to Bianca's photos and how those would rock Van's campaign if they got out. While she was still the number one person on my list for sending Bianca's photos to Van, that didn't mean Van didn't have more people who wanted to harm him or his family.

Shit.

This list of people could be huge. There wasn't any more time to waste.

"Dad, I'd like to talk to Van about the Chevaliers."

My father smiled at me before standing up from the table. "Let me grab my cell from the office and I'll call Van and ask. If I can get him on the line, maybe I can get him to talk about the Caldwell campaign commercial," he said as we all got up from the table and began cleaning up our dishes.

Mom and I had just gotten started on the dishes when Dad walked back into the room and took the dish towel that I had on my shoulder off.

"I can take over from here."

I couldn't help but smirk as I moved out of the way so that Dad could take my place. Although we had a dishwasher and had people who would help around the house, I remembered that my mom and dad would do dishes after dinner and talk about their day as a way to connect with one another.

I didn't want to intrude on their alone time, but based on how long Dad was in his office, I wasn't sure he'd gotten an opportunity to talk to Van. "Did you get a chance to talk to Van?"

Dad nodded. "I did. He gave me the contact information of his scheduler to give to you so that you can work it out around your college stuff."

"Awesome. Thanks for doing that. I hope he can help me out." I didn't elaborate though the urge to do so was there. I didn't want either one of them to try to talk me out of what I wanted to do. "Did he mention anything about the commercial?"

Dad shook his head. "He didn't say a word about it, but he sounded stressed. I wonder if it was because of that."

Suspicion crept into my mind. Was there more to it than meets the eye?

19

BIANCA

Due to the silence in the room, my sigh sounded louder than normal. I wanted to cringe, but that would admit how awkward my actions had been. My eyelids fluttered closed for a brief moment as I took in another deep breath. It was a temporary break from the reality I was facing, a small escape from the unrest that currently disturbed my life. I let the world fade for a moment, choosing to get lost in my own thoughts. When I opened my eyes back up, nothing had changed, and I was greeted by the pastel colored walls of Eta Sigma Nu's meeting room.

I sat up straighter in an effort to not show how bored I felt. Normally I would have tried to be more active in the meeting, to provide more support for my sisters, but for some reason, I couldn't concentrate on much of anything. My fingers drummed against the cold plastic cup I held that contained a non-alcoholic fruit punch, making it shake. The ice cubes clinked lightly against one another as I tried to pay attention to the report being given in front of me. It didn't work, and my mind was still a million miles away from Eta Sigma Nu sorority house.

"Are you okay?"

I nearly jumped out of my skin at the whispered question. It was Taylor, one of my sisters, and my co-star in one of the scandalous photos that was leaked to my father. I should probably tell her about what happened, but I wasn't sure exactly what to say.

"I'm good. Just tired." At least that wasn't a lie. I was exhausted from having to keep up appearances and thinking of ways to get out of the prison my parents wanted to force me into.

"Aren't we all? It'll get better and we are here for you if we can do anything to help," she whispered back, and all I could do was nod because I didn't want to elaborate.

Her words were lovely but did little to stop the storm raging in me. I nodded, acknowledging that I understood, but I didn't say anything else. I really wanted to, but the words died in my throat. Instead, I turned to focus my attention back to the front of the room.

All I could think about was maintaining my body positioning, so I didn't let on to anyone else that something was terribly wrong. It had gotten to the point that my head was spinning from the conflicting emotions crashing inside of me. The mask that I wore was doing its job because so far, no one else had tried to ask me what was wrong.

My gaze drifted and noticed that my other sisters were listening intently to the speech. While I'm sure they had their problems, either they were way better at hiding them or they truly felt carefree. If I had to admit, I was jealous because here I was, tangled up in a mess that wasn't completely my fault.

My thoughts landed on Easton, as they had over the last few days. No matter how much I tried to distract myself with things such as this, he was still at the forefront. Him fucking me again was supposed to be a distraction, but instead, it became the main attraction.

I jumped slightly, almost spilling the drink I was clutching in my hand, when my phone vibrated in my lap. I counted my lucky stars that I ended up turning the volume off, or I would have drawn more attention to myself.

I pulled out the phone and saw that it was a text from my mother.

Mom: Call me now.

I rolled my eyes at her demand to call her right this second. My instincts usually wanted me to do the opposite of whatever my mom wanted me to do, and I tended to listen to my gut. I had no intention of reaching out to her right now. Then I debated about whether I should call her back when I got to my place or if I would wait until tomorrow. I was leaning toward the latter.

After what felt like an eternity, the meeting ended, and we all started to make our way out of the room. I hung around the house for a bit, making sure that I did my best to appear to be social. I didn't feel my phone vibrate any more, indicating that my mom hadn't tried to call me back. That made me wonder how important her call was.

I left our meeting and drove back to my apartment in

complete silence. My mother's text message was weighing heavy on me, but I wasn't ready to talk to her.

I walked into the lobby of my building, my mind so focused on the text message and getting to the elevators. Because I was operating on autopilot and my attention was drawn to getting up to my place that I almost didn't hear the voice behind me call out my name.

"Ms. Henson?"

I turned to look in the direction I heard my last name being called and found the front desk attendant standing there with a small smile. Next to him was a stunning bouquet of pink roses sitting at the front desk. My mouth dropped open slightly as I walked up to the vase. I thanked the attendant as I looked around to see if there was a card with it but found none. Who had sent them?

The roses were blooming, and their color was vibrant. They smelled like freshness and heaven. A smile tugged at my lips as I leaned down to smell them once more before picking them up and walking toward the elevator.

The scent of the roses seemed to follow me as I rode up to my floor on the elevator and made my way down the hallway toward my apartment. I was still stuck wondering who sent them and why. The only person I could think of that would have sent them would be Easton because this wouldn't be the first time he'd done so. We'd talked briefly over the last couple of days about the psychology presentation we needed to make soon, but he hadn't mentioned sending flowers. It was a sweet surprise and I needed to tell him thank you.

It took some juggling, but I opened my apartment door and carefully set the bouquet on my counter. I took a few steps back to admire them again. I couldn't get over their beauty.

I jumped slightly when my phone buzzed, but this time it continued to vibrate, alerting me that someone was calling me. I grabbed my phone out of my bag and looked at the screen.

Mom.

With a deep sigh, I walked over to my couch and sat down to answer her call.

"Hi, Mom," I said and curled my feet up under me. A knot formed in my stomach as I waited for her to speak.

"Why didn't you answer my text from earlier? I've been waiting for you to reach out." Not only did impatience drip from every word, but the sharpness in her tone could cut through the toughest surface.

I rolled my eyes and tried to take a deep breath to calm the rage pulsing beneath the surface. I wished I had more time to prepare myself for this conversation with her. But unsurprisingly, of course it was all about her. I didn't want to feed into her baiting me into a fight, so I swallowed the words I really wanted to say. I didn't want any of her drama. "Sorry. I was in a meeting with my sorority. What's up?"

"I have a couple of appointments that I want you to go with me to next week."

Every alarm in my head went off because she was being vague. It was obvious that she was intentionally trying to hide something. "Where am I supposed to be going? Why am I attending appointments with you?"

"We have a couple of fittings that we need to attend."

Her words were going to drive me to the brink until I suddenly froze when realization slapped me in the face. Why did I need to go to any other fittings? I racked my brain trying to figure out why we would need to attend any fittings, but I came up empty. "I don't understand. We already have our outfits for the holiday parties I agreed to attend with you. Why would we need to go to anymore?"

"Because a new event has just popped up on the calendar." The excitement was evident in her voice, and that probably didn't bode well for me.

Of course, she wouldn't ask me if I wanted to go. Instead, she just decided that I was going already. "What event is this? I haven't told you that I'm going to anything else, and I don't appreciate you just deciding for me."

The next words out of her mouth shook me to my core.

"Your engagement party. Your father told Tristan that you were ecstatic about accepting his proposal."

Everything that I thought I knew about this situation had flipped on a dime.

20

EASTON

The piercing screech of the referee's whistle announced the end of our practice. While we had a small break since the end of the season, I was still happy to get out there and practice with the team.

My feelings were a walking contradiction and a double-edged sword because, while I was relieved that the things I needed to do for football would temporarily slow down, it was going to take some adjusting. Plus, there was nothing like the adrenaline that careened through your body when you were on the field.

As I entered the tunnel, I spotted Nash. Everything about him shouted that he was a man on a mission, and his eyes were set on me.

What the hell did he want?

We did our best to exchange pleasantries while in public and tried to make it appear as if we were cool, when we weren't. Did I miss our friendship? Yes, if I was being honest. However, a part of me didn't regret that Nash and I ended up like this because what we'd done was wrong from the beginning. It was what we deserved.

I unstrapped my helmet and wiped the sweat off my forehead as Nash stopped in front of me.

"Hey, man, great game," he said as he clapped me on the back.

I glanced at his hand on my shoulder and moved my body slightly. I couldn't help but wonder if he was doing it for show because we were in public.

"Thanks, you too," I replied warily. If he wanted to play this game, then I could do the same. For a moment, we stood there in silence as the awkwardness settled in. A version of this conversation had replayed in my head for weeks, and now it was finally time to face him.

"Can we talk for a minute?" he asked, pulling me aside from everyone else.

I crossed my arms over my chest and narrowed my gaze at him. "Now really isn't the best time."

And it wasn't. While we were slightly alone because we'd found a corner to talk in, we were still in public.

"I think now is as good of a time as ever."

I had to admit I was curious about what he wanted to say. I glanced around to make sure that we were alone before saying, "Fine. Say what you want to say."

Nash stared down at his feet, refusing to look me in the eye, and muttered, "I've been thinking a lot lately, and I don't want to keep holding onto this grudge. I shouldn't have overstepped my boundaries when it came to who Bianca could and couldn't date, because it was ultimately her choice, and I shouldn't have set you up for that fight in Chevalier Manor."

My mouth dropped open slightly as I stared at my best

friend. I was surprised by him being so open and apologizing because that's not usually how he rolled. Granted, he never turned on me until now, so I'd never been on the receiving end.

"I should have put my foot down and declined the deal because it was stupid as fuck. But I didn't want to make an enemy out of you when it was our first time meeting each other in person."

Nash nodded. "I can understand that."

"Anyway, I'm all for putting this behind us."

Nash gave me a small smile and held out his hand. I shook it, and it turned into a bro hug. Although it would take some time before things got back to the way they were, I was happy to be back on the same team as Nash versus being against him.

"So, I guess this would be the best time to talk to you about your sister then?"

Nash raised an eyebrow at me, probably wondering where this was going. "What about her?"

"I'm interested in pursuing something with her." There. I'd said it, and if he wanted to attempt to punch me again, then so be it.

"Is this something she wants?"

To be honest, I was somewhat surprised that he didn't have any idea about it.

"I'm not sure, but I plan on talking to her about it soon. I just didn't want any more shit from you. I'm being up front about my intentions, and if that's a problem for you, tough shit. Because I will fight for her every second of every day."

Nash nodded slowly as if trying to understand what I was saying. "What about her 'engagement' to Tristan Whitmore?"

My entire body grew tense when his name fell from Nash's lips. While Tristan had done nothing to me, the fact that he would agree to this charade made me want to kill him. My fists clenched and my jaw tightened as I said, "It's not happening."

Nash shook his head. "That's not what my parents think."

"What do you mean?"

"Mom called and told me that we needed to prepare for a big announcement around the time the semester ends."

I didn't like where this was going. "What announcement?"

"She'll be throwing a party that will then turn into an engagement announcement."

It hadn't been the news I was expecting, but, also, it should have been. "When?"

"In a couple of weeks."

I forced myself to take a deep breath in an effort to remain calm. "Okay. I assume my family will get invited to this party... hmmm, I need to come up with a plan."

"It probably would be best if WE came up with something. And we have to be smart about this."

It felt good for us to be doing things together again.

"I agree. My main focus is on the last challenge for the Chevaliers, and in between that, we can figure out a way to stop this whole sham."

"That sounds like a plan."

I ran through all of this in my mind for a moment before I spoke again. "I understand that you're Bianca's brother, and where you stand in her life. But if I have to blow past you in order to save her from this, I will do it in a heartbeat. No questions asked."

This time, Nash smiled at me. "I wouldn't expect anything less."

I looked around briefly before my eyes returned to Nash. "We should probably go. I'm sure there's plenty of shit we need to wrap up before we leave today."

"Yeah, that's true," Nash said as he began to walk toward the locker room.

I followed suit until we reached the place where we had to go our separate ways due to where our lockers were in the room.

"So, I'll see you around?"

"Yes, you will."

As we parted ways, the enormity of everything we needed to do stuck out like an elephant in the room. Our task weighed on me. I was a little late to the fight, but it was still a fight, nonetheless. And I refused to do anything but win.

I KNOCKED on the door and patiently waited for someone to answer. I took a small step back when I heard the front door unlocked, and Mrs. Henson greeted me with a warm grin.

"Easton! Come on in. Van is waiting for you in his office."

"Thanks, Mrs. Henson," I said in an effort to be polite. Given what I knew of how they treated their kids, I didn't want to, but I was here on a fact-finding mission.

Mrs. Henson led me down the hall and knocked on a large wooden door. I stepped into the office and was immediately taken aback by its grandeur, but I had to admit, it fit Van Henson. The walls were painted a rich mahogany and several pieces of art hung from the walls. Dark wood, including what made up his large desk and bookshelves, was also a huge part of the room. All the books on the shelves made me wonder if that was the reason it smelled slightly like a library in here, with a hint of sandalwood in the air.

Van looked up as I walked into the room and smiled warmly. I couldn't help but wonder if it was genuine or the smile he used when he was in his politician mode.

"It's good to see you again, Easton! How have you been?"

"Pretty good with the end of the semester wrapping up shortly," I responded.

He nodded and I watched a wistful look appear on his face. "Ah, yes! It's almost over. I'm sure you're looking forward to winter break." He gestured for me to take a seat, and he sat back down in the large one behind his desk.

"Before we dive into why you're here, can I get you something to drink?"

I shook my head and sat down.

"You know, I remember when I was at Brentson University. It's where I met Elizabeth after all."

Van's eyes lit up as he spoke about his days at Brentson University. He talked about the late nights he spent at the library and the classes he took. I didn't interrupt him because I hoped that him reflecting on his time at Brentson would work to build a rapport with him. Plus, it didn't hurt that he had no problem kissing my parents' asses all the time.

It was a couple of minutes before he snapped out of his memories and shifted his attention back to me. He leaned forward in his chair, placing his elbows on his desk and said, "So, you want to talk about the Chevaliers?"

"Yes, I'm about to go through my last challenge before I hear if I've been accepted or not."

Van rubbed a hand across his chin. "I remember it as though it was yesterday, Easton. The final task. It was, without a doubt, the longest night of my life. Dark. Dangerous. Above all else, it was a test of character."

I watched Van closely, partially wondering if he was bullshitting me or not. When he didn't yell just kidding, I knew he must have been serious. Questions floated to the surface, but one seemed to be the most prevalent. "What was the task?"

The older man simply shook his head. "I'm afraid I can't give you specifics. The rules are clear and state that every man's trial is his and his alone. Anyway, they might have changed the challenge since my time. What I can say is that it tested my limits. Not just physically, but mentally and emotionally too."

He paused, his eyes glinting with the ghosts of memories long past. "It was a night of self-reflection because you have a hard choice to make. I had to confront the question of what it means to be human. The fears, the hopes, the dreams, and the desperation."

A cold chill crept up my spine, but I refused to show it. I wanted to ask more, but I had the feeling that Van had said all he could. Every trial was different, so I couldn't map out what would happen that night.

Van cleared his throat, bringing my attention back to him. "You're brave, Easton. Braver than you think. You'll face your trial, just as every Chevalier before you has. Not only will you surpass it, you'll emerge stronger on the other side. Remember, it's not like passing or failing an exam. It's about discovering who you truly are."

It wasn't the answer I wanted, but I couldn't help but

think that even without admitting to any specifics outright, he'd still given me a thorough answer. Yet it was one I hadn't been expecting.

"That makes sense, in a weird way."

Van smiled and then said, "It'll make so much more sense when you go through it. I'm sure you'll receive a little bit more information before the evening of the trial. It'll help you prepare. Remember, this isn't a decision to be taken lightly. You have to think hard about what you're willing to risk, or willing to sacrifice for that matter."

I hated that his words hung in the air like a siren blaring into the night. I didn't know if I had an opportunity to back out even if I wanted to, but as much as I didn't like him for the way he treated Bianca and Nash, I knew that I had to heed his warning.

"Okay, I understand."

"That's great. Do you think you and your parents will be attending the big extravaganza that we'll be hosting here in a couple of weeks?"

I hadn't expected him to segue into this topic, but I was somewhat happy he had. What he didn't know was that I had more information about what he was hinting at. "My parents didn't tell me anything yet, but I assume they will be coming."

He smiled as he folded his hands together. "Good. It's going to be a very special occasion."

I couldn't believe he was willing to sell his own daughter into a marriage she didn't want at all. My disgust for him was growing by the moment and his small speech that he'd given on the Chevaliers felt tainted.

"It'll take the news away from some of the bad press we've been getting."

"Bad press?" I asked, wondering if he was thinking about Diana Caldwell's commercial. "From your opponents in the election?"

Van nodded as I watched anger cloud his features briefly. "You saw the Caldwell commercial, huh?" He barely waited for me to confirm before he continued. "I won't get into details, but things are getting a bit hairy, and we need to keep on our toes. Not that we weren't before. She isn't prepared for what we plan on enacting next."

I didn't have confirmation about whether Caldwell's camp sent the photos of Bianca to Van, but I was getting a small sense that Van suspected she had. I couldn't question him further on it without him getting suspicious, so I changed the topic. "I don't want to take up too much more of your time, but I have one more question."

"What's that?"

"How much information about other Chevalier chapters will I get once I'm initiated?"

Van smiled. "I like that confidence. Once you're a member, a whole new world opens up to you, including more information than you could possibly want or need."

I nodded my head as I tried to decipher what that could mean due to his vagueness. I didn't want to ask him outright about Iris, but it sounded as if I could ask more questions once I was an official member.

I just hoped that it wasn't too late.

21

BIANCA

eing in New York City for any length of time had always been a treat. Living only a few hours away and my parents owning an apartment here made it easier. My patience was wearing thin as I touched the fabric that covered my body. The sequins on this dress were too much and they were doing nothing but irritating my skin. It wasn't my style, but it didn't matter because my mother had picked it out. At least she had to cancel coming with me at the last minute because she needed to attend a charity engagement, so I didn't have to deal with her nagging in addition to this.

I felt a bit guilty as I watched the tailor fussing with the hem on the floor. She was doing all of this for nothing, I thought as I looked up and grimaced at my reflection.

This dress was supposed to be one of the options for my "engagement party" and I wanted to do nothing but scream and shout because I was being poked and prodded for no damn reason. Every tiny adjustment she made forced me to think about the reality of this party and how my new reality was closing in on me.

But this was all wrong. I wasn't going to become engaged to or marry Tristan.

It had taken me some time to come to the realization that the only one I wanted was Easton. All it took was a moment for me to think about Iris and what she would do in this predicament before something snapped within me.

"Stop," I finally said as I stared at myself in the mirror. The thought of putting on another dress and pretending to be excited about a party that was supposed to turn into one of the biggest celebrations of my life was absurd. "Just stop."

The tailor at my feet sat back on her heels and looked up at me with wide eyes. "Are you sure? We're not done yet and—"

"I can't go through with this, and it will just be a waste of time for you."

"If this isn't the dress for you, we have plenty of other options."

It was then that I realized that she had misconstrued my meaning, but I wasn't about to correct her.

"I'm sure. I'm exhausted, and we still have time to find another dress," I lied and made sure that my tone left no room for her to debate me. Trying on dresses for this party made things more real, and I just couldn't do it.

"Okay, let me help you out of this dress and then we can move on from there."

I gave her a tight smile and said, "Okay, thank you."

We took our time removing the garment from my body and once I was free, the tailor took the dress out of the dressing room, and I sat down in a chair with a huff. I grabbed my purse, which was resting on another chair, and pulled out my phone. Was it worth calling my mother to tell her once again that I wouldn't be going through with this? She'd probably berate me for inconveniencing her and tell me that this engagement was still on track.

Then an idea popped into my head, but the biggest question I had was could I make all of this work?

Instead of calling her, I typed up a text message and sent it to her.

> Me: Didn't find a dress I like, but I'm going to text Tristan to see if we can meet up.

It took less than a minute for her to text me back. It was as if she was waiting by her phone, expecting me to give her an update on today.

> Mom: Excellent! We still have time to find something. I hope you enjoy your time with Tristan!

I couldn't help but roll my eyes at her enthusiasm. She thought I was finally warming up to the idea of this fake relationship when I was doing the opposite. I moved to the thread that contained my text messages with Tristan and quickly typed out another text.

> Me: Would you like to meet today? I'm in New York City for a few hours. Sorry for the late notice.

I put my phone down to put my clothes back on, and when I was walking out the front door of the shop, my phone rang. I pulled it out of my pocket and found a text message from Tristan.

> Tristan: Sure. Come by my apartment. I'm working from home today.

Fuck. I'd been half expecting him to say that he was too busy to meet on such short notice. I also didn't expect him to say that he wanted to meet at his apartment.

It seemed like a bad idea, but I couldn't exactly think that it was a setup because, after all, I was the one who texted him. On the other hand, I had no plans of staying long, and what I needed to talk to him about couldn't be done in public.

> Me: Okay, send me the address and I'll call a car now.

He sent me the address and it turned out that his apartment was only about ten minutes away from where I was. It would take me no time at all to get there.

The ride to Tristan's was smooth, but even though I had nothing to worry about, the thoughts swirling in my mind had me on edge. When the driver pulled to a stop, I told him thank you before stepping out of the car. I walked up to the front desk, told them my name, and was escorted up to Tristan's suite on the top floor. I rang the small doorbell and waited for someone to answer.

As the door opened, I was surprised to find a woman standing on the other side.

"Ms. Henson?"

I slowly nodded my head, confused slightly by the scene that was unfolding in front of me.

"I'm Gabrielle, Mr. Whitmore's assistant. Come on in."

I was surprised that his assistant would be working out of his suite too, but what did I know?

"Mr. Whitmore had to take a quick phone call, but he asked me to make you feel at home until he could join us. Can I get you something to snack on or a drink?"

"I'll take a glass of water, if you don't mind."

"Certainly. Please follow me."

Gabrielle led me to a big, open space that reminded me of my apartment, but on a much larger scale. It was bigger and more up-to-date than the place my parents kept in the city as well. Based on where we were and how big the space was, I know that he spent a lot of money on it if he owned it.

I walked through the living room toward a door that seemed to lead out into a spacious seating area. I wanted to see it, but it was too cold to go out there, at least in my opinion.

"Here's your water, Ms. Henson."

"Please, call me Bianca."

"Bianca it is. Mr. Whitmore should be out right about..." She checked her watch on her wrist. "Now."

As if on cue, I heard a door open and saw Tristan walk out into the living room area. His stare landed on Gabrielle and remained there for a little longer than necessary, before turning to me to give me a small grin as he walked up to both of us.

"Welcome to my home, Bianca. Step into my office so that we can talk," he said before turning to Gabrielle. "Thatcher would like the reports that you and I chatted about before I had to take that call. Can you make sure that he gets them?"

Gabrielle looked at him and then down at her feet for a brief second. "Certainly, Mr. Whitmore."

"Follow me, Bianca."

I gave Gabrielle a small smile before I followed Tristan into what turned out to be his office. It was night and day from what my father had decided to surround himself with. While there was dark colored wood in the room, there wasn't mahogany to be found anywhere. Instead, he'd focused on blacks and grays along with white to outfit the space.

Once he closed the door behind me, he gestured to the seat near his desk and I sat down while I watched him walk around his desk before he, too, took a seat. His gaze on me was slightly unnerving, but I refused to show any sign of fear.

"What brings you here?"

I decided to start from the beginning of these shenanigans about this engagement party. "I assume you know about this, but my mother is planning a party where our 'engagement' is supposed to be announced."

Tristan nodded, confirming that he had. "Yes, that was why I sent you those pink roses. It was a way to thank you for making a decision."

I stared at Tristan for a moment, not sure how to say what I wanted to say. Then it hit me. "Say what now?"

"Your father told me that you were willing to go through with this whole plan."

I wanted to be angry about this, but nothing came. I felt numb to my core about all of this but was not surprised at this point that my father would have stooped this low. This confirmed that I'd made the right decision by coming here.

"That's a lie. In fact, I was coming here to tell you that there was no way that I could go through with this. I want to be with someone else, and if that means that the photos of me get leaked, then so be it."

Tristan slowly nodded, but he didn't say a word, so I continued. "It's not fair to either one of us to go through with this. We barely know each other, and I don't think this would work. As I've said before, I'm not sure of the reasons why you want to do this to begin with, but there has to be someone who would be more suitable for what you want and your needs."

"I'll make you a deal."

"You... will?" To say I was surprised was an understatement.

Tristan sat up a little straighter and then said, "Yes. This would be a whole new deal, without the engagement, and will make sure that the photos of you don't get out either."

I took a large drink from my water to buy me time to process my thoughts. When I was done, I finally spoke. "What would I need to do?"

"Bring me a story that will make the one that is brewing about your photos look like a speck of dust in this office. If you do, I'll make sure that you don't have to worry about this arrangement. Hell, if you want to leave town because of all of this, I'll make that happen as well."

Getting an opportunity to get the hell out of here and not having to deal with this party sounded like a miracle. I knew that shit was going to hit the fan with this engagement falling through, so getting out of Dodge sounded absolutely wonderful.

I licked my lips and swallowed as I tried to think of what story he could be thinking about. Sure, there were rumors about people in Brentson that circled the town, but what story would be a big enough story for him?

And then it dawned on me. The lightbulb moment that made me want to throw my hands to my mouth and scream.

"Are you talking about my father?"

When Tristan didn't make a move to confirm or deny what I'd said, I knew I had my answer. Could I find it within myself to betray my father if that was what it came down to?

Guilt tried to make an appearance, but I shoved it down, back to the depths of hell. I needed to worry about myself first, and this would be the first step. I slowly nodded my head and lifted my gaze to look Tristan Whitmore straight in the eye.

"You have yourself a deal."

22

UNKNOWN

I was protected from the cold air that seemed to engulf New York City because of the small, rustic coffee shop I'd found a free table in. The walls were adorned with a vibrant collage of coffee beans from different regions of the world, and I was growing used to the smell of brewing coffee that filled the air. It was creating a cocoon of comfort against the cold, unforgiving weather outside.

I took a sip from my now lukewarm coffee but kept my eyes strained straight ahead. From my spot at a table near the window, I watched as Bianca disappeared into the upscale high-rise apartment building. From where I was, I could see that the lobby was made of a lot of marble and the security and attendants wore what looked to be expensive uniforms. But none of that forced my focus away from Bianca Henson.

I couldn't help but wonder what she was doing here at Tristan Whitmore's building. The same Tristan Whitmore who had made his mark in the media and had more power due to his connections than any one person should have.

He had links to some of the most influential people in the city that transcended the business world.

Tristan was also connected to many high-profile politicians and Hollywood stars. It wasn't unheard of to see him on the red carpet or at a fundraiser.

But that didn't explain what was unfolding in front of me because none of this was adding up. What was Bianca doing at this building, during the middle of the week when classes were still in session? Why was she going to meet him?

That's what I hadn't been able to figure out yet.

Tossing some bills down on the rustic wooden table to pay for my coffee, I walked out of the coffee shop with my cup in hand. I pulled my coat closer to my body to fight against the chilly wind. The city's pulse echoed around me—the revving of car engines, the screeching of brakes, the hushed conversations from people around me. All of that faded into the background as I moved to see the front desk of the building from across the street. Nothing could deter me from trying to find out why Bianca was here.

I watched as Bianca spoke to the attendant there and then walked toward the bank of elevators. When the front desk attendant didn't lead her to the regular bank of elevators, I knew that she was definitely going to see Tristan.

I'd followed Bianca from the dress shop she was in for a couple of hours and then she headed here. Could it be something related to Van Henson's future political plans?

But something told me that wasn't it. The way she chewed on her bottom lip and the way she was fidgeting all told me that she was in distress. The obvious discomfort was out of place for someone who was here on friendly terms.

The elevator finally arrived, and Bianca stepped into it,

and I was left wondering how long she was going to remain in there. The city moved around me; cars whizzed by at the speed of light. Everyone was in their own little worlds, oblivious to the story unfolding in the penthouse suite above them.

I had to know why Bianca was here. I walked across the street and headed over to the building, making sure not to draw attention to myself. Blending in had become an art. When I got closer to the entrance, I noticed a security guard standing to the side near the front door of the building. Unsurprisingly, he was standing tall with his arms crossed in front of him. He eyed me suspiciously as I made my way up to the thick glass door, but he held his tongue when he saw the coffee cup in my hand.

I gave him a small nod, deciding that causing a scene wasn't the best option right now. Instead, I walked back to the coffee shop across the street to stay warm. Every step I took, I could feel his eyes on me. Once I was seated at a table, I pulled out my laptop to do some research to pass the time. Thirty minutes flew by and before I knew it, an hour had passed.

With each passing minute, I grew more irritated. I needed to know what was going on to report back. I was determined to find out what was going on between Bianca and Tristan. Tristan's ongoing relationship with Van made sense, but the connection between Bianca and Tristan didn't.

My mind was filled with nothing but questions, and I had little answers to show for it.

As the city around me continued to operate as normal, I melted back into the shadows, a specter in the chaos, with a resolve solidifying in my heart. I would get to the bottom of this mystery. No matter what it took.

After waiting for ninety minutes, the elevator doors opened again, and Bianca stepped out. She looked the same, but different. She was biting her lip again, but this time she had a determined look on her face that I hadn't seen before. She quickly hailed a cab and as she moved, I moved. When she left the premises, I was lucky enough to find a cab to follow her.

Thankfully, the cab driver I had didn't ask too many questions and did his best not to lose track of her. After about twenty minutes, we arrived at another apartment building, where I knew her parents' place was located. I waited for her to get out of the car before I turned to the driver of my cab and told him that I had another address to go to.

As he pulled away from the curb, I received a text message.

> Unknown Number: Party at Henson Mansion in approximately a week. More information to follow.

I nodded my head slowly. This meeting of two people in different stages of life had something to do with that. I was sure of it.

That was the biggest question swirling in my mind.

23

BIANCA

I stood at the front of the classroom, trying to calm my racing heart. I did my best to appear confident, but on the inside, I was freaking the fuck out. Yes, it had something to do with the presentation we were about to give, but also, thoughts of my meeting with Tristan had me almost completely distracted. Easton stood next to me, the picture of confidence as we prepared to present our psychology project to Dr. Chen and our classmates. I hated that we were the second team to present, but there was nothing I could do about that.

I looked to Dr. Chen and then she spoke. "Whenever you're ready," she said with an encouraging smile.

I shared a look with Easton because he offered to start us off and gave him a small nod so that he knew I was ready also.

"Hello, everyone. Bianca and I are here to present our analysis of the case study on Cassie Grimes, and the conclusions we reached."

On the projector screen the slide changed from just the

title of the presentation and our names to the first slide summarizing what the case study said about Cassie Grimes. Easton launched into our presentation, and together, we tag teamed, presenting the research that we'd found.

You would think, based on the fact I had to talk to strangers on a relatively regular basis because of my father's occupation, that I would be more comfortable with public speaking, but it still made me nervous.

Feeling the eyes of our professor and classmates on me, analyzing every word I said, was not what I wanted to be doing at this time. I folded my arms across my chest, and while it wasn't the friendliest body position while giving a presentation, I didn't care. I wished that I had the podium that Dr. Chen sometimes used when she was teaching because it would give me something to lean on and create a bit of a barrier between me and the crowd in front of me.

We discussed the findings of our study, highlighting the recommendations that we made as a result of what we discovered. Our words flowed smoothly, showing off how much we knew, and I made sure to talk about our methods and show off our slides which contained charts and graphs.

Everyone listened closely, and I saw some people nodding along with what we were saying. My eyes sought out Dr. Chen and noticed that she was writing some things down in her notebook, and I hoped that was a good thing.

As we neared the end of our presentation, the tension in my body released. It was as if all the stress I felt because of this presentation suddenly melted away. Dr. Chen and several of our classmates asked questions, and I was relieved when Easton and I were able to answer in turns.

Easton and I smiled at each other in relief. We did it.

Dr. Chen stood up and said, "Thank you so much for that insightful presentation. You should both be proud of the work you've accomplished."

My cheeks warmed and I knew I had a blush coloring my face. Not to mention that our classmates were clapping loudly, embarrassing me slightly because of the volume.

I had to admit that Easton and I had made a good team. We walked back to our seats and waited patiently while the rest of our peers presented their projects.

One by one, each team spoke about their projects, and I did my best to come up with thoughtful questions about the projects that resonated with me the most. Other times, I found my mind wandering about the dirt I needed to find for Tristan to keep his end of the deal.

When class was over for the day, I stood up and stretched before I turned to Easton and said, "Why don't you come over to my apartment so that we can celebrate the end of this project?"

It sounded lame coming from my lips, but I needed to get it out. I wanted to see him without it being because of school or hanging out with my brother. I wanted it to just be about me and him, and that was it.

Plus, if he was available soon, it would be before the big "engagement" night that I wouldn't be attending.

Easton thought about it for a moment before he said, "Tonight should work. I have plans tomorrow night."

I raised an eyebrow. I hated that I was wondering what he was doing tomorrow evening. I had no right to, yet I couldn't stop myself. Then it occurred to me what might be occurring. It was coming to the end of the semester and football was over, so I was willing to bet it had something to do with the Chevaliers.

"Okay, I'll send you more details about when to come over and all of that."

"Sounds like a plan. I'll see you then."

THAT EVENING, I rolled my shoulders back as I heard the knock on the door. It was show time, and I was more than ready for what tonight would bring.

I opened my door and gave the person on the other end the brightest smile that I could without a second thought.

Easton.

It was the moment I'd been looking forward to all day.

The soft click of my front door closing behind Easton sent a wave of excitement through me. He strode into my apartment, taking in the sight of the scented candles and slow soft music playing in the background.

A crooked smile appeared on his face as his gaze settled on me. "You look stunning, as always."

Warmth covered my cheeks at the compliment as I looked down at the long red dress I'd decided to wear tonight. My eyes made their way up to the navy sweater and the dark jeans he had on. His brown hair looked as if he'd been running his fingers through it. I was intrigued by the way he'd dressed because normally, I would have expected us to be in sweats or torn up jeans and sweatshirts. Yet both of us had decided to dress things up tonight as if we'd both realized how important tonight was.

"You don't look too bad yourself," I admitted.

Easton took a step closer to me and I almost stepped back in reflex because I was taken aback by my reaction to his presence in my space. "We did well today. I think Dr. Chen was impressed with our presentation."

"We make a great team."

When he took another step toward me, I moved back until my back was up against the wall. His proximity to me was doing dangerous things to my mind. I struggled to form a coherent thought that had nothing to do with us fucking right here, right now.

"That we do." His voice lowered as he reached out to push a piece of my blonde hair behind my ear. "In more ways than one."

I sucked in a sharp breath as I enjoyed the way that his fingers grazed my skin. I closed my eyes and completely embraced it. The warnings and complications about all of this faded away as I gave in to him. Easton had a way of making me forget all the reasons why I should stay away from him, but I wasn't complaining one bit.

"You're thinking too much," he murmured, his lips brushing the curve of my neck.

"I know, we are supposed to be eating dinner first and—"

"What if there is something else I want to eat, princess?"

A soft moan escaped my lips as my eyes fluttered closed when one of his kisses landed just under my jaw. How had he done this to me? The things that I actually wanted to talk to him about flew out of my mind. It felt as if it had been too long since we'd been together, and I was done with waiting.

"Then I think it's time you get to work." I leaned into him, crushing my lips against his. The tempo of our kiss was fierce, surprising even me. Not one to be outmatched, he responded by giving me the same energy. His hands ended up in my hair, fisting my strands between his fingers.

He'd set my entire world ablaze. His tongue found mine and tangled with it. His kiss was an incinerator, making me crave the feel of his body pressed against mine.

While I wanted to pretend that our movements were smooth, we stumbled toward my couch, discarding clothes along the way. He pushed me back with his body and I landed on the soft fabric of my couch. Easton came down on top of me, bracing his weight on his forearms so that he didn't crush me.

Easton kissed me again before I could think of anything else. He kneaded my breasts, massaging them before running a thumb across my nipples, causing them to stand at attention. When he licked one, I shivered once the cold air hit it. His touch stoked a fire within me that only he could satisfy.

He slid off the couch and down to his knees. I moved my legs so he could fit between them. He pressed a kiss to my inner thigh, forcing a shiver from my body.

"You're so fucking perfect," he whispered.

I wasn't sure it was something he even knew I heard.

His praise made my lips tremble as my arousal intensified. He placed a small kiss on my other thigh before guiding himself to where I wanted him the most.

My body attempted to launch off the couch the moment he touched me. It took Easton placing his hands near my waist to keep me in place. Still, even with him holding me, my hips did everything in their power to anchor his lips to my pussy, causing a groan to fall from his lips.

He took his time, paying close attention to every sound

and move I made, making sure to change what he was doing based on the cues I was giving him.

It was glorious.

I couldn't help but smile when I heard him groan. I assumed the bliss he was sparking in me was the reason why he was moaning as well. The thought of that drove me to peaks I couldn't have expected until it all came crashing down around me.

"E-Easton," I cried out as my climax took over, shaking me to my core. As the pleasure flowed through my body, Easton continued licking and sucking me. He shifted slightly just as I was coming down from the high, dragging my orgasm out. Or could he have been in the process of starting another? My brain couldn't process all the sensations flowing through me, but I knew I wanted this and so much more.

"I want you to ride this out, baby."

And I did until it felt as if I couldn't breathe anymore. My panting sounded as if I'd run a mile in five minutes flat. He kissed his way up my body before his lips landed on mine once more. I could taste myself on his tongue and it was one of the most erotic things I'd ever experienced.

When I took a moment to catch my breath, I looked him in the eye and said, "It's your turn."

I moved to make my way to the floor, but he used his hands to stop my descent. "The place I want to be right now is in your pussy. Spread your fucking legs."

I immediately did what he demanded and found him nestled between my thighs. He fisted his cock for a moment before running the tip of it up and down my pussy, coating himself in all of me. As I moaned, he thrust himself inside of me, forcing my moan to change into a gasp. I fought the urge to close my eyes because I didn't want to miss a second of this.

When my eyes met his, they were darker than I was expecting. It could have been due to his own arousal, but I couldn't deny that I saw everything I wanted, everything I needed, in them.

"You're fucking mine."

The gravity of this situation was weighing down on me, but it wasn't an unpleasant sensation. The significance of this moment caused me to feel joy and passion. It was a feeling of love.

Easton's words cut through my thoughts like a knife as he pounded into me. "I want to hear you say it."

I wrapped my legs around his waist, urging him to move faster, at the same time I placed my hands on his shoulders to anchor myself.

"I'm…" It was as if I couldn't find the words to say.

"Say it, Bianca." His words came out rushed as he picked up the pace.

"Dammit, I'm yours," I yelled as our bodies moved in a frenzied rhythm that felt as if it was completely in sync.

When the sensation began to build in my lower body, I knew that there wasn't much time before I was coming all over his dick. It was what I wanted and deserved.

"Come for me," Easton said, his voice raspy and sexy as hell. "I want to feel you come on my cock."

His thrusts became more erratic, and I loved it. With every stroke he made, I grew closer to the end, and when it finally hit, it felt as if I'd exploded.

I heard syllables leave Easton's lips, but I couldn't decipher the words he'd said as he followed me over the edge. He tried his best to keep from crushing me as he fell forward, but I patted his back, letting him know it was okay.

When he finally collapsed on top of me, I swear I could feel his heart pounding as fast as my own. Or maybe it was just mine.

Neither one of us moved, instead choosing to lay there for several minutes while we caught our breath.

"That was earth shattering," I heard him say.

All I could do was nod my head, unsure if I trusted myself to speak just yet.

The haze of desire that we'd both fell into began to lift, and it felt as if I could finally think again.

Tonight, I was willing to give to him, to give to us, but who knew what tomorrow would bring?

Easton turned us around so that I was lying beside him on my couch. Eventually we'd have to move and get cleaned up, but for now, I was content with laying right here in his arms. He reached over and grabbed the throw blanket that I usually kept on the couch and tossed it over our bodies.

"You're not getting engaged to Tristan Whitmore."

I moved my head slowly so that I could look him in the eyes. This was the last thing I wanted to argue with him about, but he wasn't about to tell me what I could and couldn't do. "That's not for you to decide."

"You know for damn sure that your body belongs to me."

His words were doing nothing but pissing me off. "Is that all you care about? Me being engaged means that you won't be able to fuck me anymore?"

"That's not what I meant."

"Then you better explain quickly."

Easton sighed. "I meant that the way your body reacts to

mine, the way we feel when we come together... you know that can't be replicated with Tristan."

I did know that he was right, but this was all more complicated than I was willing to admit. While I did have the deal I'd struck with Tristan in my back pocket, what would I do if it failed?

"There's not much I can do about this."

"Marry me. Then there is no way your parents could force you to get engaged to Tristan."

I jerked up as if I'd been hit by something and stared down at him with wide eyes. I was pretty sure I'd stopped breathing by the time he'd finished talking. There was no way he could be serious.

But as I scanned his face, there was no trace of laughter or humor about what he'd just said.

A wave of emotion slammed into me, hitting me right in the chest. A small amount of hope that had blossomed within me quickly died. With a shaky breath, I thought of a response, but almost couldn't get the words out. "I can't marry you, because you don't love me, and I don't want to marry someone who doesn't love me. You don't love me."

A bitter taste grew in my mouth after the last syllable left my lips. This was it. I didn't want a fake relationship with Tristan or Easton. I wanted something real when the time was right.

The silence around us was almost suffocating until Easton spoke once again. "But you're willing to go through with this engagement to Tristan?"

I'd been hoping that the next words out of his mouth would be along the lines of him telling me how much he loved and cared about me, but it wasn't. I swallowed my hurt feelings and said, "Let's not ruin tonight. I'll keep your suggestion in my back pocket. Okay?"

Easton nodded slowly and I was grateful for that. This could have blown up into something horrific, but I was able to keep it at bay for now.

I laid my head back down on Easton's chest and focused on the beating of his heart. It was a sound that somehow made me feel safe and secure. Despite this newfound peace, Tristan's new deal still lingered at the edge of my mind because I needed to complete my end of the bargain.

24

BIANCA

The next evening, my childhood home loomed before me as I pulled into the driveway. The sun was setting, giving the brick home an even larger than life presence as I drove up to it. I couldn't help but wonder what might greet me when I walked inside.

Anxiousness couldn't quite describe the feeling that was growing deep in my stomach, but it was close. I'd been doing my best to avoid my parents for the most part, but if I was going to find out anything about my father, it didn't hurt to go directly to the source.

Or look through his things.

I stepped out of my car and walked up to the front door. I pulled out my house key, fumbled with it for several seconds, throwing me off slightly, before I opened the door. Just as I did, I startled my mother who was walking through the hallway.

"Bianca! What a pleasant surprise. What are you doing here?" Her bright smile and friendly tone seemed fake or maybe that was my bias talking. My mother didn't do well with surprises, but I didn't care.

I'd come up with several ideas about why I would be coming home today and finally settled on one. "I wanted to talk to you about the party in a couple of days. Is everything ready to go?"

The fake smile and the tension fell from her face slightly, which was interesting. I wanted to attribute it all to me talking about something that she wanted to talk about, but I wasn't sure.

"Yes, the only thing we need to do is find a dress for you to wear. I want you to be the belle of the ball essentially."

"Bianca," my father said as he walked into the room.

Mom flashed a smile at Dad that didn't look genuine either and said, "She's here to talk about the party." She then turned to me and said, "Since you didn't like anything when you were in New York City, I had some dresses delivered to your room and I was going to ask you to stop by to check them out, but since you're here..."

I was still wondering what was going on between my parents, but I managed to say, "I'll do it in a bit. Where are you guys off to?"

I took in the beautiful ivory dress that my mother was wearing and the suit that my father had chosen to wear tonight. They both were dressed impeccably, and I had to admit, that was one of the few things they always got right.

Dad cleared his throat before speaking. "We're going to a dinner party hosted by the Williams'. We actually need to leave in a few minutes in order to arrive there on time."

"That sounds like fun." The lies were coming easier now.

This time, my mother chimed in. "It is. Your father has

been having a rough week, so an evening out would be nice for him."

Dad adjusted his tie and while his face remained expressionless, I could see the vein that appeared on the side of his head slightly bulging. He was stressed. "Did you see Diana Caldwell's latest commercial?"

I adjusted my purse strap that had fallen off my shoulder and shook my head at my father's question as I waited for him to continue.

"Essentially, she accused me of being corrupt, and there's no way I'm going to take that without snapping back at her. We have a few hit pieces that we are putting together to strike back. They'll be released over the next few days."

I didn't understand why all of this was happening when the election was just under a year away. The meetings, rallies, and speeches were picking up, but thankfully I wasn't in the thick of things because I didn't live at home anymore. What I couldn't judge my father on was wanting to respond to attacks made against him before things got out of hand and the general public turned against him.

"Do you think she has a real chance against you?"

"I'm not underestimating her. She's gotten this far by acting like she's harmless, but she's ruthless and I have to admit I admire that about her. But if I'm not careful, she could win the election."

"I understand that," I said. "I don't want to hold you guys up and make you late."

"Thanks, Bianca." My mother gave me a small smile, probably grateful that I was giving them both an out. Her weary gaze looked at my father for a long moment as he walked to get her coat from the closet.

Dad helped Mom into her coat before putting his on and together they walked to the door.

I managed to smile and wave at them as they crossed the threshold. "Good night."

It wasn't until I watched the front door close behind them and the bolt lock snap into place that I moved. The time was now, and the stakes were high. I needed to do some digging because I knew that my father had secrets that he'd buried. I was going to find them, no matter the cost.

I turned on my heel and darted down the hall to my father's office. Each step I took allowed the fear within me to creep up my spine. I was frightened about what I might find, but I had to know. My future depended on it.

If there was anything he was hiding, it had to be in there. It was his private sanctuary, where he could escape from the world and all the pressures that came with it. I didn't think Mom, Nash, or me ever entered his office without him present, not because he told us not to but because it had been an unspoken rule of sorts. And now I was breaking it amongst other things.

As my shaky hand touched the cool brass doorknob, my nerves flipped out as my adrenaline reached another level. What I could potentially find was an endless rabbit hole that I was unearthing and what I found wouldn't be able to be neatly put back inside of it. Part of me hoped that there wasn't anything to be found because if I was putting my father's dirty laundry out there, there could be some fallback on me. But if I didn't, I could be getting married to someone I didn't want to be married to.

Easton's throwaway proposal to me entered my mind briefly before I shoved it out. Distractions would only be a waste of time, something I couldn't afford to have right now. I suspected that my parents would be out of the home for several hours, so I needed to move as quickly as I could.

I opened the door and made a beeline to his large wooden desk. I turned on his lamp, illuminating most of the desk in light. Everything on the surface looked neat, not a paper out of place. As I searched through, I didn't find anything that would point to any wrongdoing, but hell I didn't know exactly what I was looking for anyway.

I opened the first drawer and found the usual. A few notepads, pens, paper clips, etc. It was as if it was his junk drawer. Nothing out of the ordinary there.

I opened the middle drawer and it looked to contain papers related to work, including papers like flyers for charity events he'd attended, books, etc. I was starting to wonder just how organized my father was.

I opened the third drawer and began to look around, when my hand landed on something weird. It felt slightly sharp but wooden, but I couldn't figure out what it was just based on sight alone. With a heavy sigh, I pulled some of the files out of the desk so I could get a good look at the bottom of the drawer. I found what looked to be a secret compart-ment. Was it normal for desks like this to have this feature in them? Or had Dad had this put in for himself? What was in it that he'd wanted to keep hidden?

I shifted the rest of the things in there and pulled on the small latch of the compartment. It pulled open with ease and I saw a manila folder in there. There was a reason he'd hidden this in the manner that he did. I carefully pulled the folder out and took a deep breath before opening the can of the worms.

It took everything within me not to yell 'what the fuck' out loud.

Emails and statements dictating that my father had been paying thousands to something called Diamond Nights.

What the hell was that?

I grabbed my phone from my purse and did some quick research.

Diamond Nights was an escort service for the wealthy.

I wasn't sure what to feel at first. My mind twisted as I struggled to make sense of what I was looking at. How could he do this? To my mother? To our family? To his career? Soon my emotions flipped from confusion to rage as anger bubbled up inside me. I knew better than to take my frustration out on the evidence in front of me.

The urge to call him and show him that I'd found all of this was here, but that wasn't the point of this expedition. Instead, I used my phone to take pictures of several of the documents in the folder.

Once I'd completed that task, I made sure to put the folder back where it belonged and put back the items that I'd taken out of the desk. I needed to make sure that I made everything look just the way it had been before in order to not raise any suspicions. I then walked out of his office and up to my bedroom where I quickly selected a dress that I didn't even bother to try on. If I did decide to keep quiet about this, hopefully the dress would fit. If I decided to blow the lid off this, whether the dress fit me wouldn't matter much anyway.

I grabbed my phone and crafted a quick message for my mother.

> Me: The dress I laid out on my bed is perfect for the party.

Without a second thought, I stuffed my phone back into my purse and left my childhood home.

I unlocked my car door and threw my things into the passenger seat. I now had the option to keep this to myself or force the downfall of not just his political career, but draw attention that would put my family in a whole different light.

I drove away from my childhood home with tears in my eyes, not completely knowing where I was driving to.

I found that I kept driving even when I should have turned my car a long time ago. But I ended up sitting in front of Soren Grant's home. I was convinced that he held all the answers to Iris's disappearance, but there was no way I was just walking up to his house to demand that he release her by myself. I was convinced that he could easily kill me if he wanted to, and that wouldn't bode well for anyone.

Instead, I started my car and headed back toward my apartment where I could finally sit down and think.

25

EASTON

Darkness surrounded me as I walked to the spot I was supposed to be. While I wanted to show that I had all the confidence in the world, my stomach twisted as I waited to see what would happen next.

The night was silent, and it felt eerie because there was no reason why the forest should be quiet given what lived out here. A faint glow broke through the darkness, as if leading me somewhere. In the distance, I could see someone standing there, and I assumed that was where I was supposed to go. As I got closer, I recognized that it was Nash surrounded by torches. His arms were crossed, and his eyes were focused on me.

"Are you ready for your final task?" His voice was cold and hard.

I couldn't help but wonder what challenge would lie ahead.

I nodded once. "I am." I felt confident about what was about to unfold because I didn't have a choice to be anything but.

"It's time to prove your loyalty to the Chevaliers once and for all."

"I'm ready. More than ready." I wasn't sure if that was a lie or not, but at least nothing would indicate that it wasn't the truth to Nash.

A wicked smile appeared on his face and was only heightened by the light from the torches. "Excellent. We've captured someone who is a threat to our chapter and let them loose in the forest. They need to be eliminated."

Eliminated? That word hung in the air increasing the tension between us that was as dense as fog. What the hell? But I stayed silent.

"There is a journalist investigating us. Getting too close. Snooping around where he shouldn't be." Nash cracked his knuckles. "If he publishes an exposé on us, it'll cause some issues, and we don't want that."

I shifted my weight as bile rose in my throat. I was supposed to kill someone? But even if I didn't want to do it now, it was already too late. If I didn't do it, the Chevaliers would kill me instead.

"Your task is to take care of the problem," Nash said, his eyes were completely cold. This was a different side of him than I'd seen before. "Everything that you need is in the storage crate next to me."

I hadn't even noticed the crate that was about a foot away from him. I bent down to dig into the box and took out a gun, gloves, a knife, a flashlight, and a rope. It might have been overkill, but it was what it was. The crate included a book bag, so I put everything in there but the gloves. Those went on my hands.

"Good luck," Nash said.

I took that as my cue to leave. The hunt was on.

I left Nash there and went further into the forest. Silence surrounded me outside of the wind dancing through the branches on the bare trees. The moon was out tonight, so thankfully I didn't have to use the flashlight yet.

I continued walking until I saw something near a big tree in the forest. Was this where the journalist was supposed to be? I turned the flashlight on and found someone knocked out against a tree.

This had to be it.

He looked younger than I expected him to, and I honestly didn't think he was that much older than me. His brown hair covered parts of his face, but I could see that he was still wearing glasses. As if he heard me, he looked up and his eyes widened at the sight of me. There was already a gag in his mouth and his hands were tied.

A slew of thoughts flooded my brain as I took in the sight before me. My first thought was that they'd made this easier for me, and I wondered why.

I shook my head slightly. How had I gone from feeling somewhat nauseous about this to wondering why the Chevaliers were handing me a murder on a silver platter?

The journalist struggled against the zip ties that held his hands together, and he tried to scream from behind the gag, but it was muffled. The noises that were coming from him were pointless because anyone who would have been willing to save him, couldn't hear him.

My determination broke through, forcing me to carry out the promise I made. I placed the bag down on the ground and unzipped it. I pulled the knife from the bag and tested its weight. I wasn't sure how much the guy in front of me could see given how dark it was in the forest.

But when I walked toward him, he jumped and tried to get away from me while shaking his head frantically. I didn't blame him. I would be trying to get away from the person who was sent to kill me as well. The closer I got, the more I could see the terror in his eyes.

"So, you're trying to take the Chevaliers down, hmm?" I bent down to his level and stuck the knife's edge under his chin. I applied pressure to the knife, drawing some blood. "It looks like I've been tasked with teaching you a lesson."

My words sounded foreign to my own ears. My threat hung in the silence, and I wondered who would make the first sound. Would it be the man in front of me or the forest?

The journalist swallowed hard and squeezed his eyes shut, giving in to his fate.

I took a deep, steadying breath and pressed the knife into his neck.

His screams were muffled, but I could still hear the pain in his voice. However, I didn't stop moving the knife until I'd pulled it across his throat. Blood fell all over my hands as I completed the motion and ran down the front of his white button-down. There was no way that stain was coming out.

His movements slowed and the light in his eyes dimmed, his head fell to the side and his glasses slid to the ground. An eerie silence fell over the forest, including the wind I'd heard earlier.

My heart slammed in my chest like a jackhammer. Had I really just done this without a second thought? Had I really just taken a human life? I'd done some shit in my past, but nothing this sinister.

After a couple of minutes, I took the knife back and stepped back from the body. My glove-covered hands had blood all over them, and I would need to take care of that. I'd completed my final task.

There were claps in the distance and I turned around to find Nash and several members of the Chevaliers descending on me. How had they'd known I'd killed the journalist?

They must have been watching me.

Nash walked up to me while everyone else stood back. He clapped me on the shoulder and said, "You completed your final task. Congratulations."

Nash's announcement led to a round of applause from the Chevaliers standing behind him. They walked forward, shaking my hand and welcoming me as a part of them. Given how serious I thought this organization was, having them smiling and clapping was a weird contrast.

Nash came back around and said, "We'll celebrate later, but first, we must do the final step of the initiation process."

Together, we all turned and walked through the forest. I wasn't exactly sure where I was going, but I was following the crowd. I turned to one of the guys next to me, and asked, "What's going to happen to the body?"

"You don't need to worry about that."

Good to know.

I looked up and saw that we were walking up to a building. Was it...

Holy fuck. It was Chevalier Manor. So that meant we weren't too far away from campus.

We entered the building from the back, and I was taken into the basement. Candles had been placed around the entire room, casting a warm orange glow around the area. On the floor was a gold design that had three swords that crossed with a crown on top, and a pair of wings surrounded the swords. This must have been the Chevaliers symbol.

Nash gestured for me to come forward, and as I did, I heard a chant coming from the men around me, but I couldn't understand the words they were saying.

"Kneel," Nash commanded.

I lowered myself down to the ground, and then Nash joined in on the chant. There was no turning back now.

Someone walked up to Nash, and he turned to his left. He grabbed what the person was holding and held it out to me. "Drink this."

I looked at the substance in the cup. I wasn't thrilled to be drinking this but took the vessel from Nash and drank the entire thing. I shoved the cup back at Nash and dropped to all fours.

"Fuck!" I screamed out as a sharp pain ran through my skull. Heat raced through my veins, and I couldn't figure out what was going on with my body. I bit down hard on the corner of my mouth, causing it to bleed. I struggled not to scream again.

The volume of the chanting rose and the shadows in the room seemed to be coming toward me.

What the hell was going on?

The pain was excruciating, and I wanted to curl up into a ball and die. After a couple of minutes, it ended as abruptly as it came. Everything became silent, and I laid on the floor, gulping in as much air as I possibly could.

"You've made it," Nash's voice broke through the silence. He didn't sound anywhere near as panicked as I felt. "The initiation is complete. You're now a Chevalier."

Applause erupted once more as Nash leaned forward and held out his hand. I stared at it for a moment before I grabbed it and stood up on shaky legs. Once again, they clapped me on the back and shook my hand, welcoming me into their family.

I was now one of them.

26

BIANCA

I gazed out the window of my apartment with my glass of wine in hand. The lights outside my window were bright and beautiful, unlike the dark thoughts in my mind. I'd managed to drive back to my building without any issues, but now I was home alone and didn't know what to do with myself besides think.

The "engagement party" was in two days, and I had a decision to make. A decision that would change my life forever no matter what I chose. I needed to figure out whether I was giving the information I had on my father to Tristan.

I ran both of my hands across my face as I weighed my options. The urge to write down the pros and cons of each option were there, but deep down I knew there was no need. I knew what I should do, what I had to do, even though, on some level, I felt guilty about it. I could try to run away on my own, but I had limited access to funds that wouldn't raise suspicion from my parents. If I took a large sum of money out and put it in my new bank account, it would set off alarms.

"Maybe I should just marry Easton," I muttered, sinking onto the couch he'd fucked me on just a few days ago. Hell, he'd proposed to me on this couch. What a mess this all was.

How could my father do this to us?

Even if I didn't go to Tristan with this information, I knew it was probably only a matter of time before all of this came out. So why did I feel guilty about being the one to leak this story then?

Because my life and my family was going to change dramatically.

Then again, it would change drastically being married to Tristan Whitmore as well.

I shook my head as I thought about all the times my father had made being a family man and the importance of family values a focal point of his campaign.

I couldn't help but wonder how many times he'd spoken those words and talked about our family but had the taste of another woman on his lips.

The most fulfilling thing would be to throw all this back in his face and watch every emotion he went through as his deep, dark secret was exposed, but I couldn't. Instead, I was sipping on a glass of wine. Although, it hadn't devolved into me drinking so much that I couldn't see straight, so I assumed that was a step in the right direction.

I needed to think more about going to see a therapist for all of this.

I placed the glass of wine down on the table and grabbed my phone. Calling Nash might be the best option and telling him about it might make me feel better. Then, together, we could figure out what we should do.

A glimmer of hope appeared in my heart as I found my

brother's number in my phone and called it. But it continued to ring and ring, without any signs of him picking it up.

Fuck.

Then it hit me that yesterday Easton had said that he was going to be busy tonight. That was probably related to the Chevaliers... which means that Nash was probably involved as well. I still didn't have an update on Iris, which I hoped to get now that Easton was likely a Chevalier.

But there was one person I could call who also had a run in with my parents.

I found her number in my phone and put it up to my ear, praying that she'd answer the phone.

"Hey, Bianca?"

The question in Raven's voice made sense. It was obvious that she was surprised by my call. She and I didn't talk too often normally and now it was becoming a habit of me calling her whenever I needed to talk to her about something troubling me. In the years that I'd known her and before she disappeared, we only really spoke because of our connection to Nash. I probably should reach out to her more often. She was a voice of reason due to her personality and what she'd been through, and I needed to acknowledge that. I made a mental note that when my life settled down I would do so.

For now though I was comforted by the fact that she was on the end of the line because right now, it was as if she was my only hope in this mess I found myself in.

"I'm sorry for calling you so late."

An unexpected calmness resonated in her response, one that I'd hoped to hear, but wasn't sure I would. "It's not a problem."

Relief washed over me, but I still felt bad about

disturbing her this late. "Are you busy?" My leg jiggled as I waited for her response.

She paused for a moment before she spoke again. "Uh, no. Is everything alright?"

"No, it's not. I just needed someone to talk to. I tried calling Nash and he didn't pick up."

"So, you called me instead."

I blew out a puff of air and said, "I hope that's okay."

"It's fine. What's going on?"

"I have a decision to make and I'm really struggling with it. I'm hoping that talking it out with someone will help me decide."

Raven was silent for a moment, making me slightly nervous. She cleared her throat and then spoke, "Lay it on me."

"I found out some unsettling information about my father, and I need to decide what I'm going to do with said information."

"Oh wow. Does Nash know anything about this yet?"

I shook my head although she couldn't see me. "I haven't talked to him about it yet. I found it early this evening."

"Okay and the information that you found out? How bad is it?"

"Pretty bad. Like enough to end this family and his political career."

"Oh my gosh... what happened?"

I hesitated, debating with myself whether it was worth telling her exactly what my father had done and then I said to hell with it. I was already this deep into it, what was the worst that could happen to me if I admitted to her what I found?

"I found out that my father has been using an escort

service. I'm not sure for how long exactly, but it isn't a new thing."

Once again Raven was silent, but this silence felt different. I couldn't quite place why this silent moment felt odd, but the longer it drew on, the more awkward I felt. I assumed it was hard for her to hear, but I needed her to say something, anything. I heard a sniffle on the other line.

"Are you okay?"

"Um," Raven started and then paused once more. The tension between us was heavy, the weight of it only made me feel awkward. I needed to say something to dispel some of it and fast.

"You're scaring me." The words came out barely above a whisper, and I hoped she would respond with something reassuring.

Raven cleared her throat and said, "I knew about your dad. He uses Diamond Nights, or at least he used to."

I couldn't control the gasp that left my lips. I hadn't told Raven the name of the company my father was a client of. "How did you know that?"

"Because I briefly thought about becoming an escort there and... I saw his name. I went to him about it, and he paid me off to leave town because he was afraid I was going to blackmail him with that information."

Holy. Shit.

"Does Nash know about this?" I asked, repeating her question from earlier.

"He does. He had a big blow up about it with your father weeks ago."

My mouth was dry, and my heart sank. This was so much

worse than I had thought. The only thing I could think to say was, "I'm sorry."

"Hey, no," Raven interjected, her tone firm. "This isn't on you, not one bit. You had nothing to do with the drama that went down between me, Van, and Nash."

"I know, but it still makes me feel like trash." I took a big gulp from the glass of wine that I had all but abandoned.

"This isn't the way I wanted you to find out about it."

"I understand that, and I don't blame you at all for not saying anything." I was torn between my frustration and my desire to have empathy for her. I wished that Nash would have said something, but there was nothing I could do about it.

"Is any of this conversation helping you out with deciding what you should do?" Raven asked cautiously.

I thought to myself for several seconds before answering her question. "Yes, actually... I think I'm going to let you go."

There was a slight pause before Raven answered me quietly, "Okay, I'll talk to you later." I hung up the phone and placed it down on the coffee table in front of me. I drank the last of my wine and replayed the conversation I'd had with Raven. She'd helped me probably more than she knew.

Because I'd made my decision.

27

EASTON

Once again, the Hensons' home was transformed, having been perfectly prepared to host the people for tonight's party. A live orchestra, with each member dressed in black, played soft music in the corner, accompanied by the muted conversations and laughter of their guests mingling in their fancy clothes beneath the warm light. There was no doubt in my mind that Mrs. Henson knew how to throw a party, and knew how to play this game well, but I hated what this one stood for.

It was supposed to be the night Bianca's engagement was announced. I glanced around and saw Diana Caldwell walking into the room. Her presence perplexed me given what she'd said about Van in her latest campaign ad. Then again maybe Van lived by the adage keep your friends close and your enemies closer. It might have also explained why she accepted the invitation and decided to come here tonight.

I almost walked over to her but stopped when I saw Nash approach me out of the corner of my eye. While things weren't back to where they were before he found out about Bianca and me, they were better. When he was next to me, I glanced at him before I went back to looking straight ahead.

I coughed once before I said, "Lovely party, isn't it?"

Nash smirked at me and said, "As always. Can't say I'm surprised to find you lurking in the corner over here."

"I'm just watching the scenery." The words left my mouth without much thought. It was mostly true. I was watching the crowd, mentally recalling names of the people I recognized. But the reason I'd come here was to save Bianca.

I'd tried to talk to her after I got initiated into the Chevaliers, but she hadn't called me back. I'd tried to make it over to her apartment earlier today, but I had to do a few things for my parents.

"You should enjoy tonight while it lasts," Nash said as he too looked around the room. "No matter what happens, nothing will be the same."

I had to agree with him, the weight of how much of a big deal tonight sank into my soul. If things went my way, things would change for the better, but if the engagement did happen, my relationship with Bianca would be over. I was worried that the latter would be happening given that I hadn't been able to contact her over the last day or so, but it wasn't over until this night ended.

I sighed again as uncertainty overtook my thoughts and the only thing that could clear it was seeing Bianca. I looked around for her once more, searching for any sign that she might have shown up, but there was none. Her entire family was here, but she was nowhere to be found.

Nash and I had agreed on a plan for me to interrupt the

announcement, but I'd made sure not to mention that I'd told Bianca that she and I could get married and that she'd turned me down. This plan would require Nash to bring attention to both of us and me having to go up to wherever the "happy couple" was standing and telling everyone how wrong this relationship was. Would Bianca be pissed at me if this were to take place? One hundred percent, yes. Was it the soundest plan? Probably not, but it beat having to murder Tristan Whitmore.

Although that was still on the table.

"Have you heard from your sister today?" I found myself saying out loud as my gaze locked onto Nash. I was holding out hope that he might have heard from her, but doubts were creeping into this situation and fast.

Nash shook his head and said, "I assumed she was getting ready here, but based on how my mother keeps looking at the door, it's obvious to me that was not the case. Plus, by now, my mother would have stormed upstairs to get Bianca because that wouldn't be the first time she's done that."

My eyes landed on Mrs. Henson, who kept looking at the woman she was speaking to for several seconds before her eyes would return to the entrance to the ballroom. I was convinced now more than ever that she was looking for Bianca too.

"Hey," Raven said as she walked up to us. She'd excused herself to go to the bathroom moments earlier.

Nash threw an arm around his girlfriend and pulled her close to his body. "Hey to you too," he said, placing a kiss on her forehead.

"I'll try to call her again," I said. Before I could turn to walk away, Nash nodded at me, but Raven looked confused about what I was talking about. I was sure that Nash would explain it to her once I left.

As I walked away, I snatched my phone from my suit jacket and found Bianca's number. When I clicked on her name, I put the phone up to my ear. It rang once and then twice before it went to her voicemail. I hated to say that I was starting to get worried.

Where the hell was she?

I put my phone back in my pocket and walked back into the ballroom. My gaze danced across the room and eventually it landed on Mayor Henson. Mrs. Henson had left behind the woman she was speaking with before and joined him. They moved across the room and ended up in a group with my parents. Mrs. Henson's stare was still shooting toward the entrance of the ballroom as if her nerves wouldn't let her look anywhere else.

Out of the corner of my eye, I noticed a slight shift in the room and detected movement near the entrance of the room, but I couldn't see who it was. I adjusted my positioning so that I could see who it was. Tristan Whitmore strolled into the room in a black suit and without a hair out of place. The expression on his face betrayed nothing. However, he didn't look like a man who was about to announce his engagement, which made me even more curious about what was going on tonight. I also couldn't help but wonder what he was thinking when it came to being the center of this spectacle tonight.

Tristan's eyes moved around the crowd as if he was analyzing the scene before him, but what was he looking for? When his gaze landed on me, he gave me a curt nod, a subtle exchange and I wasn't sure what to make of it. Was he just being polite or was there something else going on there?

I couldn't help but wonder if he knew about Bianca and me. Did he know about the things that we'd done even with this arranged engagement on the table? Did he know that I was ready to put everything on the line for her?

When Mrs. Henson saw Tristan, her eyes widened in surprise. Her gaze shifted between him and the entrance, further confirming my suspicions. I was going out on a limb here, but I wondered if the plan had been for Bianca to arrive with Tristan. Maybe a grand entrance was planned? With Bianca not arriving with him, that would raise all the alarm bells and tell Mrs. Henson that something had happened.

But what?

Without warning, the music abruptly stopped playing. The silence in the room was interrupted by a buzzing noise that started in one corner of the room and soon ringtones and alerts spread like wildfire. If I was looking down on everyone from up above, I was sure that I could have spotted the imaginary wave that I was sure crossed the room.

As if it was now my turn, I felt my phone vibrating in my pocket. Confusion followed as the crowd tried to figure out what was going on. Was this some kind of national emergency?

I pulled out my phone once more and the screen lit up with an alert referring to breaking news: Mayor Henson had been caught using an escort service.

The whispers turned into gasps as everyone in the room seemingly realized what the alert was for. The energy in the room had gone from happiness to shock in what felt like a snap of a finger. I turned to look at Nash, who was too busy staring at his phone with Raven to notice.

There were no words to describe what was happening now outside of the fact that the Henson empire, which had been a staple in this community, was starting to show cracks as if it might be preparing to fall. Everyone in attendance just so happened to be at ground zero.

28

BIANCA

I leaned back into the leather seat I was sitting in and tried my best to relax. Everything within me told me I needed to chill out, but that was easier said than done.

Was it weird to feel like I was a fugitive, escaping from what should have been my life? Instead, I was miles away from the turmoil I'd left in my wake, and I had mixed feelings about it. I was supposed to be in a showstopping gown in a room full of people, shaking hands with who knew who, at Tristan Whitmore's side. Instead, I was in a pair of leggings and my college sweatshirt, with my hair haphazardly thrown up into a messy bun.

I took a deep breath and tried to compose myself as Tiffany, the flight attendant on this private flight, appeared before me with a warm smile.

"Are you ready for takeoff, Miss Henson?" she asked, her voice calm and soothing.

I nodded my head, my heart pounding in my chest. This was it. The moment of truth. "Yes, I'm ready."

Tiffany left me alone to return to her seat, and I knew it

was only minutes before it was game time. As the plane began to move down the runway, I could feel the adrenaline that had been coursing through my veins moving to a new level. My eyes were glued to the window closest to me, watching as the world outside blurred into just a bunch of lights and colors.

I stared out the window, watching the ground fall away as the plane ascended into the sky. As the plane climbed higher, the pain that weighed me down began to peel off. A sense of liberation and carefreeness washed over me the more distance I put between me and everything that was going on back home.

I picked up my phone and found the picture of Easton that I'd taken with the intention to throw in my father's face. I was glad I hadn't done so, instead choosing to keep it sacred which hadn't been my original intention. It also served as a reminder of what we'd had before I'd blown everything up in Brentson. I put my phone down once more and looked back out the window.

It was some time before I saw Tiffany again, and I gave her a small smile when she approached me.

"Can I get you anything to drink?" Her soft voice was in slight contrast to the hushed sounds that were present in the cabin.

"Um, sure," I said, caught slightly off guard even though I shouldn't have been. "What do you have?"

"Just about anything you can think of, if I'm being honest."

I chuckled at her statement. "How about champagne?" I waited for her to ask for my ID to check my age.

"Of course," she said, nodding. "I'll be right back with that."

As she disappeared down the aisle, I closed my eyes and took a deep breath, savoring the moment.

About five minutes later, I took a sip of champagne and felt the bubbles tickle my tongue. It was a wonderful feeling. The glass was cool against my fingers. I took my index finger of my other hand and ran it across the rim of my glass absent-mindedly.

The peacefulness of the airplane cabin wrapped around me like a warm blanket. It was a welcomed sanctuary from the world outside, much like my father's office had been for him. The low, persistent hum of the jet engines was the only audible interruption that I could hear, a reminder of everything and everyone that I was leaving behind as I shifted to a now unpredictable and bumpy path ahead.

This was really happening, and I was mostly at peace with it.

I took another sip of my champagne before setting down my glass and pulling out my phone. I logged into my new bank account and saw the $50,000 deposit from Tristan. It was my safety net to spend how I wished while I was away. Seeing it there was just a reminder about what I did and how I needed to escape the scandal that was now surrounding my father.

My stomach was queasy, not from the alcohol, but from the uncertainty of what lay ahead. I'd fucking done it. I destroyed everything my family had built, and now I was on a plane out of there. I didn't know how long I was going to be gone, but I wanted to be away long enough to let the dust settle a bit before I returned.

Then again, I probably wouldn't be welcomed into my family's arms again, so maybe I'd never go back.

I leaned back and sank into the plush leather seat. Then I closed my eyes, trying to ignore the feeling in my stomach. The one thing I felt guilty about was leaving Iris with Soren if that was who she was indeed with. But me taking on the Chevaliers alone would more than likely lead to both of our deaths. Hell, maybe me being gone was best for both of us.

However, something else was bugging me. There was something I needed to know. I opened my eyes and turned on the large screen television in front of me, shattering the silence in the cabin.

"Breaking news in Brentson, New York, tonight," the newscaster said, her voice echoing through the cabin. "Mayor Van Henson has been reported to be a client of Diamond Nights, an escort service, for years, according to an anonymous source, who has provided video evidence."

My heart dropped to my stomach as the video clip played, showing my father exiting a seedy motel with a woman on his arm. My mind raced as I tried to make sense of it all. I didn't provide any video evidence, so how did Tristan get it?

Had he been holding on to this information all this time and decided that now was the best time to share it? Had the statements I'd seen just been supplemental evidence to the information he already had?

The news anchor's voice echoed through the luxurious cabin of Tristan's private plane, but I barely paid attention to the rest of what she was saying.

Watching this all unfold was almost an out-of-body experience. My whole life, I'd been groomed to uphold my family's image and reputation. Now, I was part of the reason it was being torn to shreds.

As the plane left New York behind, I couldn't help but feel like I was leaving a part of myself there too. A part that was now tainted by my father's scandal.

I was glad that I hadn't been at the party when all of this had gone down. It would have been nice to see the looks on both of my parents' faces, but for my own safety, it was probably best that I not be there.

Part of me had wanted to tell Easton what I had planned, but I knew I needed to do this for myself, alone. Maybe now I could find a way to redefine myself and my future.

Right now, in this moment, despite all the other emotions running through me, at the center of everything I was feeling, I was happy. Happy just to live in this moment of not knowing what would happen next.

THANK YOU FOR READING! The next book in the series, Shattered Reign, is available for pre-order now!

WANT to join the discussion about the The Brentson University Series? Click HERE to join my Reader Group on Facebook.

PLEASE JOIN my newsletter to find out the latest about The Brentson University series and my other books!

PREVIEW OF THE LIES BENEATH

IRIS

Continue reading for a sneak peek of The Lies Beneath.

The loud noises that were coming from the crowd fed into the energy I felt and that wasn't a good thing. This was supposed to be a minor reprieve from my daily routine and wasn't.

I hated being this nervous. This wasn't my scene but stepping outside of my comfort zone was supposed to be a good thing. Here I was at a football game watching my college's team play against our biggest rivals. I eagerly accepted Bianca's invitation to attend, but I didn't come here only to see her and to be mildly entertained for a few hours.

I wanted to get out of my dorm room and to socialize. The eeriness that surrounded Westwick University seemed to stay at the campus's gates and it felt as if a heavy boulder had been lifted off of my chest. I didn't have to worry about him.

Sports weren't my thing and me veering away from my usual haunts should confuse him. Then again, if he was following me like I assumed he was, me changing my schedule slightly wouldn't mean a thing.

It would allow me time away from his gaze that sometimes rendered me useless. Whenever I was on campus, deep down I knew that he was always there, lurking in the shadows, watching every move I made.

As I shifted through the crowd, it was nice to be just one of many. It meant that I could blend in and not be the center of attention. Then again, the purple tips of my hair drew more attention than I'd been accustomed to, but I'd done that for my own benefit and no one else's. If people wanted to stare, then so be it.

Except for when it came to him.

The way he studied me was very measured and what it made me feel was almost indescribable. I was intimidated because I could never tell what he was thinking as he stared at me. It was as if he was undressing me with his eyes, slowly peeling back every layer of clothing until he had me bare.

But it was more than that. I noticed something in his measured approach. He enjoyed making me uncomfortable, but I could prove none of this. Simply staring at someone wasn't a cause for concern, but it should be when it came from him.

My professor.

And my stalker.

How I'd ended up in this situation seemed to have happened by chance, but the more things happened, the more I wondered if it truly was a coincidence.

I forced myself to look into the crowd to see if I saw Bianca.

This was the first time in I didn't know how long that I didn't feel as if he was anywhere nearby.

And then it happened. My entire body felt as if it were on edge, and that meant only one thing: He was here.

I could feel his presence in this stadium full of people. That sounded strange, I knew, but I also knew what this feeling was. I'd grown accustomed to him being in the same vicinity and the slight shift in air was there.

The coldness in his eyes sent a shiver down my spine even though I hadn't turned around to find out where he was today. No, I wouldn't give him the time of day.

Instead, I saw my friend's profile and walked straight to where she was sitting with another woman.

"Bianca?" I asked although I was pretty certain it was her. When she turned to face me, a wide grin took over her entire face.

"Iris, hey!" Bianca quickly pulled me into her arms before I had a chance to react. When we broke apart, she gestured to the woman standing beside her. "Iris, this is Raven. She's my brother's girlfriend. Raven, this is my friend, Iris."

"It's nice to meet you," I said as we shook hands.

"Likewise," Raven replied. "I'll move down and you can sit on the other side of Bianca."

I'd never heard Bianca mention Raven, but she seemed pretty adamant that we should meet and this was a perfect opportunity to do so.

I could feel him watching my every move as Bianca and Raven moved so that I could take the seat they were saving. As we got settled in our seats, I looked up and saw Raven look behind us and pause. That was when I knew she'd spotted him.

I hated that my instincts were right in this case. I debated saying something, but what was there to say?

No. I couldn't say a word.

The ringing of Bianca's phone snatched our attention and I was relieved. It would save me from having to speak on something that could mean life or death.

Bianca shrugged her shoulders and showed the message to me before she handed the phone to Raven so that she too could read the message. I stared into space for a moment as I recalled what the text message had said.

> Unknown Number: Be careful what you wish for, B.

My initial reaction was to tell Bianca that we needed to report this to the proper authorities, much like she'd been begging me to do again when it came to Soren. It would be beneficial to have detailed records about what was going on. But I refrained selfishly because of my situation. It made logical sense for me to report Professor Grant to the cops and to the president of Westwick University. But when you're dealing with a man with as much money and power as Professor Grant, you're walking into a world of trouble and hurt.

Speaking of him, I took a deep breath and looked behind me. Professor Grant was nowhere to be found.

ABOUT THE AUTHOR

Bri loves a good romance, especially ones that involve a hot anti-hero. That is why she likes to turn the dial up a notch with her own writing. Her Broken Cross series is her debut dark romance series.

She spends most of her time hanging out with her family, plotting her next novel, or reading books by other romance authors.

briblackwood.com

The Lies Beneath

The Truth Between

The Shattered Trilogy

Shattered Saint

Shattered Sinner

Shattered Reign

www.ingramcontent.com/pod-product-compliance
Lightning Source LLC
Chambersburg PA
CBHW061437210726
48287CB00007B/2253